Before the Past Escapes Us

by

William H. Adams

Words Matter Publishing
P. O. Box 1190
Decatur, IL 62522
www.wordsmatterpublishing.com

ISBN: 978-1-953912-86-2

Library of Congress Catalog Card Number: 2022940744

DEDICATION

This book is dedicated to my late grandmother Dorothy L. Adams. I know you're somewhere smiling down on me, thank you for looking after me for so many years and believing in me when I could not. Also, I dedicate this to my fiancée Faith La Rue who I am so grateful for every day of my life. Without these two wonderful women, this book would have only ever been a dream.

TABLE OF CONTENT

PREFACE

Within the pages of this book are a collection of short stories that I had written over the past few years of my life. Writing is something I have grown a passion for ever since I was a child and it truly is a dream come true of mine - for my words to be seen and read by the whole world. These stories range across many different genres that span from horror and suspenseful tales that are all too commonplace in our society today, to stories akin to the realism and romanticism movements during the 19th century. There is also a diversity between the stories I tell. Some, such as "Diary Of An Anorexic Boy" are told from my own personal experiences that I have dealt with throughout my rather short but eventful life. Other stories, such as "What the Blind Man Saw", while a good work in its own right, have come directly from my imagination alone. You may notice during the course of reading that many themes and ideas seem to be intertwined with those from another story in this collection. This was not a mere accident, as I intended to carry over some of those themes to my other stories to show perspectives that I had not previously discussed. For example, the characters from “The Bridge” are the same characters that appear in “Happy Face”, although told from a different speaker. Finally, I chose the title *Reflections* for this collection because I believe this is what drives the narrative throughout this book. The characters in these stories will commonly reflect on something profound that they have learned, and I hope that you, dear reader, will have the same reactions when reading.

WHAT THE BLIND MAN SAW

I used to think I had everything I could have ever asked for. I had a well-paying job and I was loved and well respected within the community. The whole world seemed to be in the palm of my hand before I met him.

Now, I recall this day quite well. Just like any other day, I walked along the downtown sidewalk without a single care in the entire world. That was, until I passed a man. Not just any man, mind you. I truly believe that this man was quite wise, perhaps well beyond his years. However, this did not replicate this man's fortune. Quite frankly, the man had none to speak of, which led him to begging just for survival.

I just about passed him completely without a second thought about it. It was he who spoke up and asked me, "How do you do, good sir?"

I could only groan internally before I answered him. I turned to look at him with the most fake smile plastered across my face. "Quite well, I must say, and yourself?" I politely asked, truthfully not caring one way or another how this man was doing.

"Well, my friend," he began, "I've not been doing very well at all."

I paused, not sure of how I was supposed to proceed further with this conversation, if I even should at all.

I became angered with myself as I sat next to the man, for I thought I should be going about my day and not spending what time I had with this complete stranger. Yet, in my heart for some strange reason, I could not leave the man alone, for I sensed that he needed me. "So, what are your troubles, mister?" I questioned him as I tried to get more information as to who this man was and why he was here.

The man merely chuckled to himself, making me sure this was nowhere near the first time someone had asked him such a question. "Well, let me answer that question with one of my own," he said.

I recall sitting on the sidewalk quite perplexed.

The man continued with his question. "When you look with your eyes what is it that you see?"

I paused for a moment. "I'm sorry sir, I'm not sure I heard you right," I politely told him.

"Well young man, the question is quite simple. When you look around what is it that you see?"

Perplexed, I wondered if the old man's question was more rhetorical than one that had a definitive answer. "I--I don't know what it is I see," I answered bluntly.

Now this was much to the amusement of the old man as he chuckled yet again at my response. "Come on fellow, tell me what it is you see."

I looked at the old man for a second and his face gleamed with excitement. I decided to amuse him for at least a little while longer. "Well, I see some buildings," I began rather blandly. "There's a lot of people walking around and going about their day. I see many cars both parked and driving past us." I observed the surroundings to my newfound friend.

"Is that all you see?" the old man spoke up.

"Well, I'm not sure what it is I'm looking for exactly," I told him honestly.

"None of us are, but I implore you to look again. I feel that you're a lot closer than you may think," the old man said to me.

I felt as though he was trying to tell me something that I couldn't understand. At this point, I could not allow myself to leave this old man. Even though he was merely a stranger, I found myself consumed by his words and wondered what exactly it was that the old man wanted me to see. I closed my eyes while I took in the deepest breath I had ever taken. When I opened my eyes again, it was as if I had entered a completely new world.

"Now what is it that you see, friend?" he asked me again.

"I see flocks of birds as they soar across the sky. It's as if they do not have a single care in the world." I felt the man grab hold of my hand and with an ever so tight squeeze, he told me to go on. "I see a wonderful bed of flowers in front of us. They're tulips I believe…yes, yes! They have to be some of the most gorgeous that I have ever seen before. All of them are alike, yet quite distinct in their own special way."

I described it to the old man and perhaps I piqued his interest as he asked me, "What color are they, young man?"

It was at this point that I had realized something about this man. He was absolutely blind! Stunned by this new discovery, I was left speechless for a few moments.

Eventually this caused the old man to speak up yet again. "Are you okay friend?"

This was all it took to snap me back into reality. "Oh, yes, of course! The flowers are yellow, the most beautiful shade of yellow if I must say so myself." After I said this, I looked over to the old man who had the largest smile on his face.

"Like the sun?" he asked with a hint of childlike wonder.

"Oh yes, very much so, I would say."

"Please tell me more," the old blind man asked of me.

"I see some trees to the right of us. The leaves are absolutely beautiful this time of year, oh so much green! And my goodness, I can't remember the last time I've seen such tall trees! I'm sure the kids would have a field day trying to climb these, or maybe it's the perfect home for a little critter." As I told him these things, it brought so much joy out of the man.

"Yes, you have quite a good sense for detail my friend, it's as if I can almost see the scenery for myself. It's something I don't believe I've felt in many years," he told me, and as I looked at him, I noticed the tears flowing down his face, not tears of sadness, but it seemed, tears of absolute joy. "Is it as beautiful as I believe it to be?" He asked me curiously.

"Yes sir, even more so. I'd say it is truly breathtaking." We sat together, hand in hand, and for a mere second it was as though this magical experience would last a lifetime. But unfortunately, as is the case with any experience, none can last forever.

We conversed for a while longer, talking about the sights and sounds that surrounded us. We told each other about our life stories. We must have sat there all day having the time of our lives. That day is one I will always cherish and remember for the rest of my life. The day that I found the true beauty that surrounds life itself. A beauty that we sadly fail to take advantage of, a beauty that's left quite underappreciated by humanity.

Everyday thereafter I would walk down that same sidewalk, always sure to take the time to appreciate the beauty of nature around me. The birds, the flowers, the trees, are some of God's finest creations, and because of this old blind man I can now appreciate them as God intended.

As I walked down the sidewalk I'd see my wise old friend, whom I would always take the time to greet. We talked about everything from the color of the flowers to stories of our childhood. Just like with nature, I felt my bond with this man grow every single day.

That was until one day, when the man was no longer there. Another day passed and still no sign of my friend. This happened for weeks until one day, I began to hear rumors around town of the old blind man's death. Coincidentally, his body was found on the sidewalk, exactly where the man and I became such good friends. From time to time, I'm still left thinking of that man, and what he either intentionally or unintentionally taught me. While he may have been gone for a long time now, his lessons and his spirit will live on forever in the nature that he desired to see the most.

THE CHARMING CANNIBAL

It's with great possibility, while it fills me with regret to say this, that I may have gone insane. I first noticed this months ago, although at this point it feels like an eternity, a never-ending hell, if you will. It was her lovely face that had originally caught my evil eye. I believed this kind of beauty was to only be found in fairy tales, and yet, there she stood before me in all her glorious flesh and blood.

I was quite infatuated by her presence, so much so that I began to watch her through the coming days and nights. The more I chased her the more I inevitably fell in love with her. Now for a disclaimer: I am not, nor have I ever been, nor will ever be a stalker. I did what I did merely for love and love alone, which some may say negates the idea of "stalking" as any kind of offense. I would continue to watch her for weeks as I would begin to take notes on her routine, who her friends were, what shops she chose to go to, etc.

One day I finally acquired the nerve to introduce myself to this lovely woman. My natural charm and charisma were able to kick in. We talked for a while, and I could feel our chemistry growing by the minute. She was blissfully unaware as to how many times the two of us had seen each other before. Oh, how ignorant she was, never having the slightest idea as to what would happen next.

I ended up inviting her to dinner that night, something I rarely ever do but there the two of us were. We formally told each other about ourselves, while the various things she told me were all things I had previously found out about her throughout the prior weeks. When it came time for me to tell her about myself, I could not bring myself to be truthful to her. I lied through my teeth, but the smile on her face said, *I believe you. I trust you*. After what had seemed like never-ending small talk and a few too many drinks, we left the restaurant.

We found ourselves in the cold and dark streets, just the woman and me. "It's getting late, perhaps you would like to stay at my place tonight?" I asked her.

She paused without saying a word, which left me quite worried that all my hard work would prove worthless in a matter of seconds. The thoughts scurried through my brain so fast that I almost did not hear her say, "Yes, I'd love to."

I took in a sigh of relief as we found ourselves back on track. We arrived at my house. I locked the door to assure that we would be left uninterrupted that night. The thoughts previously in my head alone had become my reality at that moment.

"You have quite a nice place here," she said, which once again awakened me from my thoughts.

"I appreciate you saying that! Could I get you anything to drink?" I asked her.

"Just water will do me just fine," she said with a smile, that beautiful smile.

I went into the kitchen to get her a glass, yet my eyes kept wandering to the set of kitchen knives nearby. I picked one up and looked at the sharp blade as my curious face reflected off of it. *No, not her. She's different from the rest of them,* I thought to myself. It has quite frankly become an addiction of mine, the absolute desire for some flesh and blood. While I must admit many women entered this house before never to be heard from again, this one was special, special in the sense that she deserved life. I put the knife down as I knew that the longer I held it in my hands the more likely it was my demons would take over.

I entered the living room once again to greet the guest, who still appeared to be oblivious to the danger she was in. We chatted for a while longer and my heart raced all the while. She told me her dreams and what she wanted in life, and I… I continued to tell her untruthful things about myself. Perhaps in that moment I felt ashamed for the things I had done in my past. How do you tell someone your deepest, darkest secrets and not feel fear for the consequences that come with it?

I wanted to tell her that the place, and myself for that matter, were not safe for a woman like her. I continually bit my tongue, however, my heart rate became faster and faster with each word that came out of her mouth. Eventually, she inquired as to where the bathroom was. I notified her that it was the first door on the right and she walked away leaving me with so much relief as well as pain. Relief that I could finally breathe, yet pain in that she was still breathing. *You're doing the right thing. You're a good man,* I attempted to reassure myself.

Just when I had almost talked myself out of the situation, I heard a blood-curdling scream arise from the other room. How could an angel so beautiful make a sound so awful to the ears? I jumped to my feet in a hurry to discover the absolute horror which had fallen upon the young woman. Instead of opening the door on the right, she had accidently opened the one to the left. Normally this would be a simple mistake, but for her it wound up being deadly. Inside the room to the door she opened, there was memorabilia here and there from past victims, so I could never forget the horrors of what I did to those women. Even more unnerving for her, I'm sure, were the skeletons of these past women, which were scattered across the room from head to toe. She turned to me with a look of absolute horror on her face as she asked, "Who are you?"

Now, I never intended for her to find out this particular way. However, at this point, I couldn't have allowed her to leave if even she desired to. She rushed past me as she tried to make a run for it. I caught her just in time as she reached the exit. I tackled her to the ground with all I had in me. We hit the ground hard and the two of us began bleeding profusely from the impact of the concrete floor beneath us. I began thinking to myself that this was the most thrilling experience I'd had in ages, quite possibly ever. Yet, I was then brought back to reality with a slap to the face and a knee in a place I would rather not mention.

She was quite the fighter, but it only takes one hit to kill you. I ran to the kitchen to get my knife for in the face of almost certain death, she still remained strong. I looked into her eyes and for the first time it was not a look of terror I saw, but one of pure anger and frustration. I never had this much trouble with such a task before and I felt as if perhaps I was losing my touch. We tussled some more as each of us tried to dodge the other's incoming attacks. Then, I stopped thinking. I let my limbs take over instead which proved helpful when I slashed her directly across the face. It angered me to see how much she was bleeding. So much good nutrition gone to an absolute waste.

I couldn't stop myself from cutting and stabbing her even more. My addiction took over all sense of logic that I had left. I looked into her eyes again while I did this, and the anger I saw earlier was now gone and replaced with a much too frightened and sorrowful look. Just how I like it. It only took mere minutes for her to pass away. I became more filled with remorse as reality slowly began to hit me. Was there any time for me to reflect on the past? No, not when I still had so much left to do. I began the preparations as I reminded myself of how long it had been since I was fortunate enough to have such a delicious meal. Part by part I cut her up until she was completely unrecognizable. As I cooked, I began to drool at the mouth, and I felt my animal instincts come back.

It was hours later when I finally could eat my meal. It tasted quite bittersweet in a way, as while my cravings were finally satisfied, I couldn't help but feel much guilt in the pit of my stomach. Guilt that she never got to live a full life while a mad and bad man such as myself lived on. However, I didn't think about it too long as I retired to my room hoping that a good night's sleep might ease my mind. I turned the lights off, which just left me with my demons to battle through the night. At least, that is what I had believed at the time. I began hearing a voice calling out to me, although the message was quite mumbled. "Hello? Who is there?" I asked as I sat myself up.

The voice became clearer, this time saying, "Why? Why did you put me here? It's so dark, I'm scared, please get me out of here!" I paused momentarily until I began to decipher who the voice belonged to. "You're not real! I killed you myself! The dead cannot speak!" I shouted to the bodiless voice before me.

"But I am! I do speak, for I speak to you and only you." The voice explained to me, "I still feel so much pain, the way you cut me up and forced me to die. That pain will never be able to leave me!" the voice continued. It was then that her lifeless body had come out of the shadows of my room. "You must pay for your sins, not only the ones you did to me, but for all the women whose fate was to meet their end by your hands!"

I hid under my sheets in absolute horror, hoping that this was some form of nightmare that I had imagined. Yet, what was occurring was all too real. The ghostly woman yanked my sheet which left me exposed to the horrors I'd so strongly tried to avoid. When I looked up, it was not just one figure I saw, however. There were dozen of them! As I looked at their faces, I saw ones I could recall quite well, along with others who looked only vaguely familiar.

"Look at us. Look at us and weep!" "You should recall my fellow lost souls," the ghostly woman said. "Do you remember Janine?" I was asked by her, but my mind drew a blank. "Janine was only in her twenties when she met you. She had so much promise with so much to give to this world. She was an artist, who would live and die by her art, and you took that away from her! She can no longer paint or draw for she was destined to become one of us, lost souls who have no hope for redemption.

"No, no, no! That can't be true!" I cried. "I didn't mean any harm towards you women, you must believe me!" I desperately cried to them, only to be greeted with the collective yelling of "Liar!" It occurred to me somewhere around this time that I was no longer in control of the situation.

"You will hear all of our stories until you pay for the crimes you committed against us all," the ghostly figure in the middle demanded.

"Please just let me go," I begged of them, with tears flowing down my face. However, these ghostly figures had different plans for me.

"Oh, no, no! There's still so much for you to see. Do you recall Annette? Such a loving creature she was," the spirit in the middle told me.

I looked to see which figure could be the Annette in question as my eyes stumbled on the weeping figure with quite the solemn look on her face. I figured this was Annette, but I could not in all honesty remember anything specific about her.

"Annette was a loving mother and wife. She held so much joy and pride in the life she had made for herself. That is, until you took that away from her. You took advantage of her and murdered her in cold blood!" the woman explained to me.

"I'm sorry! I'm sorry to every single one of you! Please speak to me no more, I need some rest!" I cried to the women.

"If you are sorry, then why not admit to it? Her daughter had to grow up without a mother, an entire family is broken. Did you know it's been five years and they still list her as missing? But I know where the body is!" The ghostly figure giggled with delight as I began to hear knocking from the hallway. "You should get that. I'm sure it's very important." The figures, one by one, all began to laugh at me. Not a laugh brought on by something humorous but from absolute madness by these women. The figures dispersed and I was left with this loud and obnoxious sound of knocking that was haunting me so! I attempted to sleep through the noise, but this soon proved unsuccessful as the knocking grew louder and more urgent.

I slowly got myself out of bed and tiptoed my way down the long and dark hallway. I found myself becoming more and more unnerved with each step I took. I stopped at the door to my special room which truly seemed to be the center of the horrid knocking. Time was standing still as I looked at this door, becoming frozen with fear from not knowing what was behind it. Although I was quite scared, I was driven to feed my curiosity as well. With caution, I grabbed the door handle and with a deep breath I threw it open. To my surprise, it was as if a tornado had made its destructive way through the room. There were papers, pictures, and clothing all scattered about in this mess that once had resembled a sanctuary to me. I looked upon this destruction and cried, for what I had spent my entire life's work on was now a useless mess.

I felt more sadness and guilt than I thought was ever possible on that day. So many of these memories of my victims were scattered on the floor. These women who could have once lived full and happy lives, now reduced to nothing by my cruel hands. I finally understood why those women had tortured me so, and I figured then that it was truly much deserved. As I realized this, I felt a cold breeze come across my neck which gave me goosebumps. I turned to see the ghostly figure which belonged to the most recent poor soul to encounter me. In her hand was a knife of which, upon further inspection, proved to be the same knife I had used just hours ago to end her life.

We did not utter a word to each other, for our stares into each other's eyes said all that was needed. She handed me the knife which had once slain so many poor women. *Not anymore,* I told myself. I clenched the knife as tightly as possible and stabbed myself in the chest. The knife punctured my heart and I fell to the ground. In my final moments I reflected upon my life, and how much harm I had caused. As I lay on the floor gasping for air, the figures surrounded me once again as they all witnessed my pain. I saw so many smiles on their faces, and in that moment I realized that, after years of pain and suffering, they were now free. That realization was the last thing I thought about when I took my last breath seconds later. I must plead with you to not feel sympathy towards me, for everything that occurred in this story I brought upon myself. Moreover, you should feel sympathy towards the women I had murdered and their spirits who still roam the Earth to this very day.

THE SLEEPLESS NIGHT

The clock strikes twelve as the wind blows hard and loud outside of my house. I hear the tree branches tap, tap, tapping on the glass window. My paranoia continues to grow as the floorboards annoyingly creak. The sounds of terror follow me everywhere. I open my eyes and ears. Why can't I find a sense of peace and quiet? Why can't I just go to sleep?

The clock strikes two as I stare at the darkness where once was my bedroom ceiling. The ticking and tocking of the clock only gets louder and faster the more I think about it. But I cannot stop it, my mind chooses to run a million miles an hour in my head. Even though I am tired beyond belief my mind continues to think, creating scenarios that shall keep me awake. I'm caught too much in the pain and grief that surrounds me. What a tragic story it is to be an uneasy mind with no rest or sleep.

It's now four, a night unexpectedly turned into a never-ending chore. With only my thoughts to converse with, the night has led to being such a bore. I have to get up in another three hours, five minutes and twenty seconds. Now nineteen... eighteen...but who's really counting anyway? Please, I'm begging whatever is causing my lack of sleep to just allow me to call it a day. To rest my head on my pillow and leave this cruel world is my only form of escapism. Yet, the frightening sounds are still well and alive.

The clock will annoyingly keep time moving forward, as I battle with these demons and become distracted by these hideous sounds. The ticking, the tapping, the creaking, have all made my night a living hell. For hours upon hours I've been distracted from my dreams as these noises grow faster and louder.

I take in one last deep breath, which has proven quite calming. Then I listen…nothing…no sound whatsoever as they have left my mind. I can't help but allow a large smile to come across my face as I listen to the silence that surrounds me. Finally, I get to close my eyes.

Finally, I can get my desired sleep. Although this is cut short by the sound of my alarm clock blaring which signifies the start of a new day. Once again, I cannot escape the noise. I let out a sigh and I turn the alarm off and proceed to bury my head in the pillows. The new day for me is much the same as the night previously, but there's always the chance for tomorrow, right?

Right.

THE DEMON COMETH

Walter is dreaming late one night of a very solemn shadow. This is to say "shadow" because it does not represent anything we know to be a person at all, nor does it represent any being we've ever seen before. The shadow it creates is accompanied by a shovel and body bag in its hands. The shadow drops the bag carelessly and it begins digging into the ground. This nightmare is enough horror to wake any person from their slumber.

He hears knocking coming from his bedroom door, and with curiosity killing him, goes to answer it. "Fiona, do you have any idea what time it is? I'm trying to sleep in here!" He says grumpily, thinking his sister is the cause of this noise. He opens the door to find no one at the other side. Not even his cat, who had a tendency to claw and yell outside of his door late at night. Walter checks to his left and his right one more time for assurance and again, nothing is there to greet him. Put off by this, Walter adds it up to something he had thought up himself from not being fully awake yet and decides to return to bed. The knocking comes back once again but this time Walter just stays in bed, confused by the occurring events.

The big wooden grandfather clock rings eight times, signifying the morning hour. After a night of getting little to no sleep, Walter blankly stares at whatever morning cartoon is on the television. He is soon greeted by his little sister Fiona, who has been taking care of Walter for the time being after a nervous breakdown he had suffered earlier last year.

"Good morning, Brother," she says with a caring smile. "My goodness, are you alright? It looks like you are dying," she observes.

"I feel like it, too," Walter jokes, without even moving his eyes from the television in front of him.

"How long have you been up?" Fiona asks her brother.

"I can't really remember," he says with a look of discomfort on his face. There is a long and awkward pause between the two of them, both suddenly quite unsure as to what to say.

"Please don't forget your next therapy session is today at two. I'm sure that will help you out a lot!" Fiona speaks up, trying to lighten the mood by acting hopeful.

"Yeah…sure thing," her brother says, but the confusing events of last night mean that Walter does not actually listen to a word his sister says as he is stuck in thought. "I'll see you tonight and I love you!" Fiona says as she rushes out the door to another busy day of work while Walter gives her a fake smile in response.

He has been left both physically and mentally alone with the absence of Fiona, the only one who is left to worry and care about Walter. Walter turns back to watching the television, which distracts him from the shadow of his dreams standing right behind him.

The appointment fails to go much better this morning. "How long have you been having this dream?" his therapist asks Walter.

"I don't know. At least a few weeks, probably more."

"And how does this dream make you feel?"

"How does it make me feel? Well, how do you think it makes me feel? To feel like you're being watched every day, but you don't know by whom or what?"

Walter begins to become more unruly as he continues to talk. He doesn't want to think, let alone talk about what's been going on. Would they even believe him? Would they understand him? They would probably just think he was crazy, which might not be too far off the mark.

"Maybe it would help to draw what you have been seeing and feeling. That way it might be easier for myself and others to see what you're going through," the therapist suggests.

"I mean, I guess I could try it out doc," Walter says with a hint of sarcasm in his voice.

"After all, sometimes the best way to get through our demons is to make them visible to the naked eye," the therapist says, or at least that is what Walter believes as he looks up to find not his therapist sitting across from him, but instead the very shadow of his deepest and darkest nightmare.

"What's wrong Walt? Everyone must face their demons sometime in their life," the shadow says with maniacal laughter, almost mocking Walter.

Walter's heartbeat begins to race astronomically; his eyes begin darting around the room. He cannot take it anymore and Walter dramatically flees without once looking at the therapist or the dark shadow he represented.

"Walt, wait! I'm still getting paid for the full hour, right?" the therapist yells to no one since Walter has not only left but closed himself off from the outside world.

Walter races down the halls and is greeted by many shadows from every direction he attempts to look. This becomes too much for him and he runs as fast as he can to the safety of his car, trying to forget about the demons that are haunting him.

He returns to his 2011 Malibu and immediately rests his head on the wheel in a mixture of relief and fear. However, once he looks up to the mirror, he can see the shadow sitting in the back seat, staring at Walter coldly. This causes Walter to speak to this being for the first time as he shouts, "I don't know who you are, or what you are, but please, I'm begging you to just let me be! I can't handle this torture anymore! I just want my life to have some hint of normalcy!" Walter begins to cry as he hits the steering wheel out of frustration. He looks at the mirror again and this time the shadow has once again vanished, leaving Walter to decipher reality for himself.

Walter has now returned home and has begun practicing his drawing exercise like his therapist had recommended. An idea, mind you, that Walter considers to be stupid, however, he complies out of helplessness. Once he's finished, he takes a moment to look at the picture. Its haunting eyes beamed a bright red, the stare it created could leave anyone with chills. Its body, which was quite unhuman-like, only made it more scary as the figure towered over the other parts of the image.

Walter becomes overwhelmed yet again as he is alarmed by the return of the rapid and furious knocking he had been the victim of earlier. He looks around the entire room, constantly unsure of where the sound is coming from, leaving him quite fearful. Walter throws his notebook across the room as hard as he can, along with the unnerving drawing it contains. The knocking continues and Walter curls up into the fetal position with the thought that this may be the end of him.

Alas, the knocking stops once he hears that ever-familiar voice. "Walt?" Fiona asks, the worry evident in her voice. Walter looks up at her and quickly attempts to compose himself.

"Hey sis, you're home early."

"Well not exactly, it's eight in the evening. I had to run a few errands. I apologize."

"What?" is all that Walter can say. He is sure that just a few minutes ago it was a quarter after five. He looks up at the trustworthy clock, and lo and behold, the time had indeed just struck eight, much to the confusion of Walter.

"I guess I must have lost track of time…"

"Well at least you've been keeping yourself busy. How was therapy?"

"I don't know."

Fiona looks at him, frustrated. Then, in a stern voice, "Well Walt, at least tell me you went!" "I did, I did!" Walter begins defensively, worrying that his sister might be upset with him. "It is just very hard right now. I wish this was something that I could explain to you," he continues. "Then do Walter, I'm your sister! You shouldn't have to keep these things from me, I just want you to talk to me about what's been going on," Fiona says in a motherly tone of voice, as she cared for her brother deeply. Walter walks over to his notebook and hands it to his sister as he symbolically opens up not only his mind but his heart as well.

"What are these things, Walter?"

"I think they might be demons."

"You think?" Fiona scoffs after saying this, not yet comprehending what all of this could mean.

"The therapist said it may be a good idea to draw out what I feel so people could see the world through my eyes. Or something like that." Walter had obviously been only half paying attention to what the therapist had said during their session.

"These are horrifying…but you don't actually *see* these monsters, do you Walt?" Fiona asks him, still quite confused. There is a long and awkward silence between the two of them, in which Walter fails to even look his sister in the eyes.

"Walter, you need to answer me." Fiona demands in a stone-cold tone, indicating how serious she had become.

"Yes, I see them, in my dreams most nights," Walter admits nervously.

"So that's all this is, it's some recurring dream?" his sister says with relief.

Walter stands and begins to leave, obviously not taking too kindly to what Fiona said. "I don't think you're getting it."

"Then help me Walter, please! I want to help you."

"You're not my mother so you might as well stop acting like it." Walter slams the door with all of his might, prematurely ending the conversation between the brother and sister.

Fiona is left to ponder to herself over what had happened between the once inseparable siblings.

Walter lays in his bed, understandably upset over the interaction with his sister that occurred only minutes earlier.

Before Walter even notices, the shadow appears next to him, however this time it finally speaks. "She thinks you're crazy," it says in a dark and cold voice, one of the most terrifying that Walter had ever heard.

Walter takes one deep breath in and tries to converse with his demon. "Maybe she is right. That's why you are here I presume?"

The shadowy figure gets closer to Walter and speaks cryptically. "I've always been here with you. I've stayed motionless and silent for far too long, just until the time was right."

"What's that supposed to mean?"

"Well, I see that you need me, child. After all, I feel everything you feel as well as see everything you can see. You could say you and I have become somewhat one and the same. So you ask what I mean? I mean I want to help you get your life back on track. I want to protect you."

"You're lying to me."

"I've never been more serious in my life," the Demon assures.

"Then who are you here to protect me from?"

Just as Walter asks the question, a knock is heard. It's his lovely sister, attempting to make amends for their disagreement earlier. "Walter, are you in there?" Fiona asks

Walter and the shadow both stay silent and motionless on the bed.

"Well, I just want to say I'm very sorry about what happened earlier. I shouldn't have stepped out of line like that. Please come out and talk to me brother, I'm quite worried." She pleads with her brother, to no avail.

Walter still does not move and is seemingly unfazed by what she is trying to tell him.

With a frown across her face, Fiona begins to leave, but not before telling Walter, "I love you."

Walter mouths the words back to his sister as she leaves.

Walter pouts as the shadow points out in an antagonizing tone, "Even your own sister is against you. How alone you must feel."

In defense of his sister, Walter decides to use his voice. "I would think I was crazy too. She has more than enough reasons to think that. I can't blame her for that."

The shadow laughs at what Walter says, almost as if he knows something our apparent protagonists do not. "Oh, but you can, and you will in due time," the shadow says as he vanishes once more, which leaves Walter alone to ponder over what just occurred.

He grabs his drawing from earlier and begins tearing it into pieces until it is utterly destroyed. Walter shouts angrily as he throws the remaining pieces of the paper into the air carelessly, before he breaks down and weeps. There is no one to comfort him, for he is all alone.

After a long and quite difficult night, the morning sun greets Walter as the new day begins. He wakes up panting and in a sweat as he once again relives the nightmare of the shadow. Walter props himself up, and looks around to make sure no one, or rather, nothing is there beside him. He goes to the living room, only to hear Fiona on the phone.

Letting curiosity get the better of him, he hides behind the wall while his sister continues her conversation. "I'm just really worried about him, Mom. I think it's about time we took him to a facility for a while, so he can clear his mind," Fiona suggests to their mother.

Walter feels betrayed by this, he doesn't want to be abandoned by his family and put into the care of a medical facility. However, he takes this news silently so as to not be heard.

Fiona continues speaking with a sense of defeat in her voice. "The two of us have not had a meaningful conversation in months! I'm afraid I just can't help him the way a professional could."

Walter still stands behind the wall, becoming angrier the more words come out of her mouth.

"I'll give it a little more time but if nothing changes then I don't think there's any other choice. Yes, thank you. I love you," Fiona finishes as she hangs up the phone.

Walter hurries back to his room before he is noticed by his sister.

Fiona sighs from the pressure she is under as Walter's mental health continues to deteriorate.

As he returns to his room, he immediately succumbs to a panic attack over the news of his potential departure, leaving enough opportunity for the shadow to rear its ugly head yet again.

"I told you that she cares not for you. She would much prefer if you were out of her life for good."

"She's trying to look out for me," Walt says in an unsure voice.

"If she were looking after you, you wouldn't be in this situation to begin with."

"Stop it."

"You're on your own, Walter, but you don't have to be anymore."

The shadowy figure puts out his hand for Walter, however he does not accept.

"Shut up!" Walter yells, having had enough of the shadow.

"You just need to let me in and all of your problems will be…" the shadow is cut off as Walter throws glass at the shadow, causing it to vanish.

"I said shut up!" Walter yells to no one in particular.

Before he can become filled with relief, his sister knocks on his door. "Walter are you okay? I'm hearing a lot of noise there," she asks her brother worriedly.

"I'm fine, sis! Something just fell over," Walter says untruthfully to her.

"Oh…well okay, dinner will be ready soon," Fiona says, not believing a word he had said, but too afraid to confront him after what had happened last night.

Walter gives his thanks, and Fiona leaves just as the shadow reappears.

"You lied to her."

"Well, it would not be the first time."

The Demon cackles, saying, "I always knew you had a sense of humor."

Walter stands up and yells at the shadow angrily. "Well apparently you do too since you can't seem to stop messing with me!"

"Your anger is not necessary. Everything I do is for a greater purpose," the shadow assures his prey.

"What greater purpose is that?" Walter asks curiously, to no response from the shadow. "Okay, be that way. I'm going to dinner." Walter says as he walks out of the room, the shadow smiling all the while.

Walter and Fiona now sit at the dinner table sharing their low budget meal together. Given that they are on tough times with only Fiona working they cannot afford the same quantity or quality of food as they had previously. "What's going on?" Fiona finally breaks the silence. "You have barely even touched your plate," she observes.

"I guess I am just not that hungry," Walter says, not looking at her at all.

"Walter, you need to eat," Fiona says, her motherly instincts kicking in.

"I know I should," Walter replies through gritted teeth.

"Then what's stopping you?"

Angered by this question, Walter slams his hands on the table. "Stop interrogating me!" There's a heavy silence as both process all that's occurred in the past few nights. "I think I need some fresh air," Walter mutters with his head down in shame as he walks out the door.

Fiona is left alone, questioning what had happened to the sibling she used to call her best friend.

Early the next morning, Walter has returned home after a night of drinking all of his sorrows away. He stumbles his way through the house, trying to not wake up Fiona in the process. He knocks into a bookcase, spilling books and knickknacks all across the floor. A light then turns on, and Walter is greeted by the voice of his dear sister. "Who's there?" Fiona asks tiredly and she rubs her eyes profusely.

"Hello sister!" he says, obviously drunk.

"Walter, do you have any idea what time it is?"

"Well not precisely, I forgot my watch."

"Are--- Are you drunk?"

"No, of course not!"

Fiona has had enough with that remark, "Walt, I can smell it on your breath!" She says in a tone that would lead one to think she felt quite betrayed.

Walter merely stares at her with the blankest expression, knowing that he has been caught red-handed.

"That is it, I'm calling Mom!" Fiona says as she walks away from her brother.

"Why?" Walter asks, though deep down he fully knows why and just cannot admit it to himself.

Fiona grabs the phone and explains her motives, "Why? Because I've had enough of this, Walter. I've tried to take care of you for months and now…well now I just can't bring myself to do it anymore," Fiona bluntly says.

"Fiona, I need you to calm down," Walter pleads with his sister to no avail.

"You need professional help, Walter. You haven't eaten or slept regularly in months. To add to that you're also always talking to yourself!"

Walter grabs his sister's arm and tells her, "Please Fiona, you can't do this to me. I just need one more chance. I promise you I've just hit a rough patch."

But his sister is not having it as she yanks her arm away from Walter. "You've been in a rough patch for almost a year now Walter. I'm sorry but it's the only thing I can think of to do at this point." Fiona's voice is filled with both sorrow and remorse. She does not want to do this to the person she loves most in life, but she can't let him keep living in paranoia and fear as it takes a hefty toll on his mind.

Fiona starts to dial the number, but Walter grabs her more forcefully this time as he pushes her against the wall, basically holding her hostage as he pins her to the wall. The phone falls to the ground between them, the number left undialed before Fiona could call for help.

"You're not going to call that number!"

"Walter, please stop. You're scaring me!"

"I don't need help...I don't need help!" Walter doesn't know if he is saying that to his sister, or more importantly telling himself that he does not need help.

Fiona is finally able to get free as she punches her brother, giving her time to run away.

Walter runs after her, gaining closer and closer to her with each passing second. This chase only happens momentarily before Walt is able to grab her by the staircase. "What was that?" he asks, feeling disgruntled.

"I was getting the hell away from you! I hate to tell you this Walter, I really do, but you have not been yourself in a very long time." Fiona speaks from her heart.

Walter looks away to contemplate, however, when he looks back he sees the devilish shadow in place of Fiona. "No…I told you to leave me alone!" Walter yells with fear in his voice and horror on his face. The shadow stares back at him, not saying a word, or so Walter thinks, as Fiona stands before him, confused by what her brother is going on about.

"Calm down."

"Get away from me, you demon!"

"What are you talking about? Walter, come on..." Fiona grabs Walter, however, he still thinks she is the shadow.

This causes Walter to hit his sister as hard as he can, taking out all of the frustration he has been building over the past year.

Fiona falls down the stairs due to the devastating blow from her own brother.

The sounds of her stumbling can be heard by her brother as he falls to his knees. Thinking that he has finally slain the shadow, Walter looks over the staircase and is suddenly slammed back to reality as his sister's lifeless body lay at the bottom of the stairs. "Fiona?" is the only word that escapes Walter's mouth as he rushes to her aid. He sits next to her and for what will be the last time, he holds Fiona in his arms. Walter howls as he realizes what he has done.

He hangs his head low and says a prayer for his fallen sister. Walter sighs heavily, knowing now what he must do. He wraps her body up inside a garbage bag, taking one last long look at Fiona's beautiful and lively face.

Walter walks outside with the bag and a shovel in his hand. He finally realizes what his nightmare meant, knowing it wasn't a nightmare at all. It was something real, it always was. It had been a premonition - someone or something trying to warn Walter of the horrors that he would soon experience, these omens that he had refused to heed. He arrives at an empty plot of land in the backyard, perfect for hiding something. He digs and he digs until his arms can hardly move anymore. He looks down at this abyss of an empty hole as his heart begins to sink.

This is nowhere for my sister to rest, Walter thinks to himself. *But…* he thinks again, *but where else is for her now?*

With great care, Walter places his sister into the hole, her eternal resting place. As he covers the grave, his fears seem to be covered up as well. The only feeling that remains is that of sadness. Sadness for loss of both a loved one and of one's true self. Walter contemplates everything as he finishes covering the grave, leaving not one trace that a burial had occurred just moments previously. Walter leans down and recites the Lord's prayer to his sister's memorial, a prayer that was also her favorite when she was living and breathing. With a heavy heart, Walter finishes his prayer and rises once again, only to see the shadow, which had been silently looming behind him, unseen and unheard.

Fiona, Fiona, how I had loved you so. Fiona, Fiona, I'm sorry you had to go. I try to block out the noise as the screams grow louder. There's no more freedom of choice as the demons in my mind become stronger. "Best to leave all hope upon entering here, for there is no chance of returning as the world around you keeps on burning," they spoke to me.

Fiona, Fiona, you're always close to home. Fiona, Fiona, outside lie your bones. The fire around me should burn my skin but it makes me feel more alive. The temperature continues to rise and rise and rise until I cannot so much as think anymore. I can no longer feel remorse or guilt for what I had done, this makes me feel like a monster, devoid of any sense of morals.

Fiona, Fiona, such a beautiful soul. Fiona, Fiona, I shall love you more than you ever will know. For I still look out upon your burial site, and I feel nothing, even when I try so hard to feel something. Your time has come too soon, and now I'm left alone as I ponder over who truly deserved to be the one to die.

Fiona, Fiona, please forgive me for I may never forgive myself. Fiona, Fiona, I will join you soon and we can embrace within each other's arms for all of eternity. You looked so peaceful in your rest that I just could not help but smile for now you can no longer feel pain, and soon neither shall I.

Fiona, Fiona, your soul shall fly to the heavens above, while I pray that I do not fall down to the unknown abyss of hell for my sins, where I will live with my crimes for the rest of eternity and you hopefully may rest with an easeful mind.

THE BOXER'S TALE

As I step into the ring, I become terrified. I stare death right into its glaring eyes. They are the hungry eyes of a strong fighter. I can practically feel his fists clenching tighter. The packed crowd is on its feet, the fans cheering to their hearts' content. Yet I don't hear them for I am too caught up in the overall emotion that this ring contains. Not only from me but from my opponent as well. We are both in desperate need of a win, a win that tragically only one of us is destined to possess.

The ring of the bell breaks my train of thought. My opponent charges at me with almost primal rage. He swings at me to the left, right, and the center. I began to question what hell I had gotten myself into. His flurry does not let up as my defense grows weaker. I'm clearly outmatched in this battle. This is no average fighter, he is 280 pounds of absolute muscle, which beat me out by an easy 150 pounds. His height I would estimate was near 6'7" causing my opponent to tower over me. If you were to ask anyone in the arena, I'm sure they would tell you that he had this in the bag and quite honestly after the punishment I've received here today I'm inclined to agree with the crowd.

I can feel the blood dripping down my face. My suspicions are confirmed as I look to the ground to see the red smeared across the mat in such an ugly manner that it would cause even my mother to faint. I had fallen onto the canvas with such a hard impact that for a moment I was sure I had been knocked unconscious. There is a lot of noise in the arena, so much so that I find it hard to even hear the referee shout, "1…2…3!" He has started the dreaded ten count, and I can tell from the look on his face that not even the man who is supposed to be impartial has faith in me right now.

"4…5…6!" The referee continues, his voice filling with doubt. I try to move my body but to no avail. The crowd is roaring at me in disapproval, some even in laughter. My opponent does not find this amusing, however, as his glance never once left my vicinity. Even with as much confidence as this man has, he is still a professional fighter through and through. Therefore, he waits, ready for his prey to rise to his feet so he can finish me off.

"7...8...9!" The referee calls out to me and after that, I'm on my feet. I do not know how I was able to make a comeback so quickly, but you must believe me when I tell you that it felt as though my body was moving on its own, not corresponding with my mind whatsoever.

I'm stumbling around as I wonder where I am. In all honesty I cannot recall the name of the venue or even the town that we are currently in. But I can tell you that I recognized this ring all too well. I bounce off the ropes without giving a damn as I figure that to survive this has to be my only plan against such a strong opponent. I hit him hard over the head again and again, with about as much force as that of a frying pan. I can't give up and I won't show this fighter even a second of weakness anymore because now things are personal, and I've begun to feel alive again. So, I keep on punching, and I never once let up until that beast before me can no longer stand up.

After one particularly vicious blow to the jaw, my opponent fell hard to the mat. I look at his face and see all his fresh wounds and old scars, some from me and some from those who have had the misfortune of fighting this man before. "1...2...3!" The referee begins the count as I observe my opponent. He looks like he's out of it, much like I had been only minutes prior. It feels quite odd for the roles to be reversed so quickly, yet my father always used to say how much life was full of miracles. Given the situation I feel as though the word "miracle" is fitting to my fight, and I'm sure many in the crowd are beginning to agree.

"4...5...6!" I can't believe that I've done this. My heart is racing dangerously fast simply at the idea of tasting victory. I've never gotten this close before, let alone against such a fearsome opponent.

"7...8...9!" He looks as if he was dead. Then, I hear the referee shout it with such surprise, "10!" The crowd erupts into cheers as they all witness the unthinkable happen along with me. "He's the miracle kid!" I hear one particular child shout excitedly. The referee raises my hand and I'm finally left to soak in the glory that I've given my blood, sweat, and tears for.

Even though the fight was brutal and gruesome for both of us fighters, I think it proved something about us. Yes, in this ring we are filthy animals out for nothing more than fresh meat. But there is more to it than that, it's the emotion and the feelings I get from it. To hear the crowd chant my name for the first time in months assures me that this battle was not fought in vain. I used to think that boxers were cursed with nothing more than fighting for the winner's purse but there's more to it than that. Sure, I receive the winner's purse at the end of the night for my victory, but the true reward is the lesson I learned from this fight. That is, we're all just different souls amidst a countless number of different battles but in the end the brightness of humanity will shine through. My father taught me that long ago, and in a way that little kid in the crowd taught me that as well.

I look over at my former opponent as he stumbles to his feet. I walk over to him and extend my hand to shake his. I wanted to let him know that just because I beat him didn't mean I was better than him, I was far from it as a matter of fact. Moreover, I wanted to let him know that I respect him. The feeling was apparently mutual as he embraced me in a hug. "Thank you," he said. "That was the hardest fight I've had in a while." He grabbed my hand and raised it as high as he possibly could. The crowd roared loudly in approval as we both took in a moment of victory, in what would later become solidified as the greatest fight of my life.

STARRY STARRY NIGHT

The stars burn so bright in the sky on this dark and lonely night. It makes me feel a sense of wonder when I lose myself in the night sky. As I contemplate many things, the demons haunt me all the while. Just about my whole life it has been either do or die as I run through the roadblocks in my life. Yet I won't give up, I'll keep going and take what's mine. I'll join my friends in the night sky.

And the Song of Life sings:

"Everyone needs dreams, to keep them moving on
But what do you do, when you realize your dreams are gone?
No longer allowed to sing your swan song."

Yes, I'll be flying high with the stars in the sky, even if it be the last thing I ever do. I continue to reach and grab all that I can but they're all so far away. The stars mock me along my pointless journey through life. Maybe I never had what it takes? Maybe I'm just stuck playing it safe? How much longer until I absolutely break?

I cannot let myself give up even if I fail continuously, it is better than never trying at all. So, I keep reaching for these stars and I keep falling harder and harder with each attempt at glory. I pick myself up, I tell myself I can't give up. I must admit I'm broken down, yet unbroken is my heart. So, I keep going until I can grab all the glorious and wonderful stars.

And I sing my song all the way, saying:

"Everyone needs dreams, to keep them going on

But what do you do, when you realize, your dreams rise with the dawn

Leaving you forever grateful to sing your song."

DIARY OF AN ANOREXIC BOY

Entry 1: April 14, 2011

Today when I was at school, I got called fat. Everyone laughed it off as some joke but to me it's something that meant much more. I just want to feel accepted like all of the other kids, they get to play and have the time of their lives during recess while I'm stuck inside. Because they don't want to play with me, they don't think I can run as fast as them and that I can't swing just as high but it won't change the way I look so is there even a point? I can be the best at every single playground game and still I would likely be ignored because I don't look like them, they think I look too "funny". I'm inside some bathroom stall crying because I'm not comfortable in my own body and hearing that word said just makes it even worse. Why must we put so much value in tearing each other down? More importantly to me, I want to find out why I was born this way, so ugly and hated.

Entry 2: March 2, 2013

I look at myself in the mirror and I'm left disgusted. Is this really me? No, no it must be some mirage that my mind has brought upon me. Either way I question why my reflection haunts me so. I feel uglier than I ever have been, and I can feel my anxiety building up by the day. All of this because I was called fat. Isn't it funny how words can stick with you? I just want one person to tell me I look good so that maybe I will believe it just like I believe all the mean and awful jokes that are directed my way.

Entry 3: May 12, 2014

Today will be my last day at this school. In a way this is a relief because I know I won't see half of the people in this room ever again. Is it wrong for me to feel delighted by this? I want to like my peers so bad but it's hard when they put you down just to feel better about themselves. I feel my clothes clinging to my body, showing off my grotesque figure. I hate this, I hate the thought that everyone is looking at me and laughing to themselves in secrecy. I don't think I'll ever truly figure out what makes someone look "funny", and I don't want to at all. I want so badly for everyone to be accepted and loved for the way they are. Sadly, our world cannot treat its inhabitants in such a way.

At the end of the day, I look to my yearbook only to find no signatures. Not from my classmates or my teachers or anyone else. How do you think this makes me feel? Well, it makes me feel alone and forgotten, almost as if the past eight years I've been to this school have been for nothing. No one will remember my name and I doubt that any of them care about that, but I do. I care because I will be the one who has to remember my classmates and all of the hurtful and nasty things they said about me behind my back when they thought I could not hear them. I always did but I let them continue because what is there for me to do? Should I tell a teacher how I feel unsafe in the classroom? Well, I already tried that, but my complaints fell on deaf ears and the bullying continued.

Entry 4: June 22, 2014

As the days and the weeks and the years go by, I will try to forget all that was said. I still remember and so these words will follow me until my deathbed. Let it be noted that I don't hate these people for all that's been said and done, although it's better to say I try not to. But I'll always question why? Why do humans find humor and comfort in the belittlement of others? Weren't we all made from the same flesh and blood? If we were, shouldn't we all treat each other like brothers and sisters as opposed to enemies? Why knock someone down, who's only trying to stand up on their own two feet? These are the questions that I continually ask late into the night.

I've been losing sleep and weight, but most importantly I've been losing myself.

Entry 5: August 27, 2014

I decided that if people were to want to be my friend, I must first change the way that I look. Over the summer I've been struggling every day. I tried and succeeded in losing the weight that was the constant basis for ridicule at my expense, thinking maybe I would be more liked and well respected if I were to look better. I work out constantly, I eat very rarely, and this builds my confidence. As my family members tell me, "You look good," it makes me feel like for the first time in a long time, people notice me. I've even made some new friends, who have no idea of the demons I have battled in my past and that comforts me. Because they never saw me at my weakest, they only see me now. A much more beautiful me if I do say so myself.

Entry 6: March 14, 2015

I've gained weight. I hate myself. I'm a monster. This scale must be lying to me, as is this mirror! Gaining weight means that I lost self-control and in turn lost my body that I have worked so hard for! I can't go back to my old self anymore, I'm much too content with the life I have now. I've gotten more attention and affection than I've received in my entire life, and I just can't lose that. I look at this mirror as it taunts me. It angers me so much and I've finally had enough. I clenched my fist and punched it through the mirror, which shattered into bits, just like I had done before. I pick up the shards and what do I see? An ugly reflection, the reflection of me. But that part of me is dead now, I got rid of him just like everyone else had previously. He's trying to scratch and claw his way out, but it does not change the fact that he is and forever will be dead.

Entry 7: June 24, 2015

How could this have happened? This unbearable pain in my stomach that makes me feel as though I'm dying. My family took me to the hospital and to be honest they didn't know what was wrong with me. I didn't either. The physician had me step on the scale and I read that fateful number that said, "82 pounds." I haven't weighed so little since I was merely a child. Now I'm a growing teenager, but maybe I should not use the word "growing" as that doesn't apply to me.

I'm shrinking in my waistline and in the joy I experience in life. "I've never looked after a boy with anorexia before." I hear the nurse tell my mother out in the hallway. I'm not anorexic, the very idea of such a thing is quite ridiculous. I'm okay…I will be okay.

Entry 8: June 26, 2015

What a couple of days it has been. I've come to terms with many things, although do not for one moment think this means that I am happy to be trapped here. I'm now not even allowed to eat in privacy, always having someone watch me for "my own personal safety". I think it's weird. There's only one other person in this place, a girl looking to be a little older than myself who went by the name of Patsy, whom I admired and respected. We constantly talk to each other to pass the time and I am learning so much, like how she had been in this ward of the hospital multiple times previously because of her battle with anorexia, which I'm beginning to come to terms with myself piece by piece. Patsy was one of the first people that I believed to not have judged me upon my looks alone. She cared more for my personality, and so we got along quite well. There's just the two of us in this prison that's supposed to help us become better, but I don't think the program made me feel better. I believe that she herself did that alone. She looked like me in that she was little more than just skin and bones, just like I was. It made me realize that maybe I am sick and that's okay. I went back to my room, forced to lay in my bed for the rest of the day, and it gives me time to reflect, time to think about what is really important in life. It can be quite lonely here at night, but at least I have some life lessons to take away from this experience.

Entry 9: July 2, 2015

The nurse said I get to go back home today. Although they are not allowed to disclose my weight to me in fear that I may relapse, she's willing to tell me that I am getting much better than when I had entered this dastardly building. I'm aware that I needed this experience but do not for one second think that it was a happy time, for it was not. Other than the one hour a day I ate with Patsy, I was alone in my room with nothing to do but pick up writing. After all there's only so many times you can watch the same sitcom reruns again and again. So I was quite relieved at the opportunity to step outside for the first time in weeks.

During my last meal, I had a long talk with Patsy. She told me about how happy she was that I get to leave and be free once again, however this is not a privilege she has. She must stay here, sadly, making me all alone in this cruel world yet again. I gave my goodbyes to her and the nurses who had taken care of me and without looking back I stepped out of the building that to me represented a prison cell, in that I had to face repercussions for my actions. But I also learned a lot, I think, for example I now know the importance of one's true self worth.

When I stepped out of those doors it was like the beginning of a new life for me. As the sun shone down on me, I felt free and more alive than I had in years. I couldn't say a word, I could only smile in relief that I learned such a valuable lesson, relief that I may learn to walk around as someone who loves myself. I look up to the window to see Patsy waving back at me proudly. I can just barely make out the words, "You did it!" coming from her lips, something that I can only smile in response to.

I don't think I'm ever going to see Patsy again, nor will I likely step inside that prison again, but the memory is something I cannot and will not let go of. For if I do, it would mean that I forget everything that I've learned about myself. I still think about her a lot, wondering how she is doing. These are questions that I have not the answers for, but I learn to accept it. Just like how I learned to accept the act of moving on with my life. I learned to accept anorexia nervosa and the broken souls that make up that group of people and it's something I'm proud of now. Because I've proven how much of a fighter I truly am, the fighter that seemingly insignificant girl saw in me to begin with.

THE GRAVE DIGGER

As the clock strikes midnight, and the full moon begins to rise, I'm tasked with digging a grave amidst a cold and dark night. The deeper I dig, the more I think about. Who were you when you were among the living? Who were you? What song did you sing? I look to the tombstone for answers; however it is nothing more than a blank slate, no name, date of death, not even a list of family members who had passed on prior to this poor soul.

I keep reflecting on these thoughts as I stare into the dark void that is this six-foot-deep grave I made for you. Your eternal bed is now ready my friend. You've seen all there is to see so I now lay you down, so you may rest in peace. As I fill the grave up yet again, I begin to feel this sense of loneliness, like the departure of this corpse has led me to sadness. Well, how can this be? I've never had any issues whatsoever with my job, but this one is different. This one has a story to tell, I just know it.

A story that is destined to be heard and eventually forgotten about by time. Just like every other body that has graced the underground, they lived on borrowed time. Just like I do now,

I suppose. It makes me question whether I lived my life to the fullest. Sure, by society's standards I am proven to be quite useful, as without my job the dead would not have someone to give them their final resting place. Yet, to me nothing I do has any purpose. I grew up with many dreams; I wanted to be a writer, a poet, as a matter of fact.

But dreams die out just like these corpses, so I am left with a dream that I never got the chance to fully pursue. I accepted this job because it was what I was told I should do and not because it was something that I wanted. I continued with this for years while always staying silent as to my true wants and desires for my career. I felt like if I was destined to become a renowned writer then whatever spiritual being that exists would give me a sign, something that without a hint of doubt would be a sign of my true destiny.

Could this be the sign that I have waited so long for? The feeling in the pit of my stomach tells me that it is time to pursue the things that I love in life. I could breathe for the last time any day now so why should I wait to pursue my dreams? I've done my fair share of waiting and now is my time to succeed. I shall send in my notice to the employer in the morning and then I will begin my life anew as I always intended it to be. Perhaps all dreams do not die out, merely they stay dormant waiting for someone to act on them.

It's weird to think that any day now I could be joining them all down there. There's something truly eerie about that. Yet also, it encourages me to live every day to the fullest before it's too late. I walk around the nameless graves one last time as their caretaker and wonder when I'll become one of them, and then, will my story ever be told again? If my story is destined to be told for the rest of time, then I must make it my absolute duty to make it a good one.

THE BRIDGE

We used to see him every day as he walked around with a smile on his face. He had the knack for making friends with almost anyone with his charm and wit. He would laugh and dance and sing with so much joy and glee as he would face all the problems that life would bring. If you needed something fixed, he would always be the first one to lend a hand, and if you were down in the dumps, he could cheer you up in a matter of seconds. He was truly the pride and joy of our town. He was quite the hard-working man, and he loved everyone without a doubt. The only exception to this rule was when it pertained to himself.

He was happy, right?

Of course, he was happy! The thought of his nice smile hiding any amount of sadness sounds absurd, his smile was so genuine. Besides, if he was not happy someone would have surely noticed. Why wouldn't he have had a happy life? He had everything a man could ever want. He had a nice house and a well-paying job to go with it. This man was successful by every stretch of the imagination!

He was happy. Alright?

I was there on that fateful night, I must tragically say. I saw the good man jump off the bridge into the cold winter waters below. I yelled and screamed for someone to help him but by this point most of the town had retired for the night. By the time an ambulance was able to arrive at the scene, he had already given his last breath. He had frozen in the cold winter waters until his body could not take it anymore. If we would have known something sooner, maybe then we could have prevented this. If he would have said something, then the whole town would have been there for him in an instant. However, perhaps he did tell us in his own special way and we were merely too ignorant to notice. No, because then we would have to live with the grueling thought that we had somehow played a role in this. It's better to not dwell on these thoughts too much however, as only one man truly knows what events transpired to lead up to this, and that man, that amazingly great man, left this world far too soon.

He was not truly happy, and that's not alright.

HAPPY FACE

My heart mourns for a simpler time. It weeps away in pure agony. But the smile across my face hides the shame. When times get tough, when life gets rough, I can only smile through and through. Some may call it a poker face, others may say acting, but I will let you in on the secret: it's neither. My face has just become so accustomed to this fake smile that it has now become a part of me. Is it a lie? Yes, but it's one that I'm comfortable with.

I smile ear to ear as it eclipses all my darkest fears. Fears both big and small, reasonable and absolutely absurd. All who pass by me are not giving a second glance as if to ask, "What's wrong with him?" They can't. Because I fit in, I'm just like everyone else on the surface. I could not possibly reveal my true self, that person is far too weak for a public setting.

So yes, I do admit that I put on this mask of a happy man day in and day out. Because no one needs to know what it is like to sit all alone through the night and cry once you're out of sight. It's a harsh reality that many are just not ready to face yet, the reality of mental health. They don't understand that not everyone who looks okay is actually okay and I'm not going to be the one who ruins that self-made stigma for them.

I shall continue to weep my nights away then, largely unbothered by everyone else. This process has become quite routine at this point. No one is here to console me or to even listen to me. That's good, I don't need that. The only person who needs to know how messed up I am is myself, and I fully intend to keep it that way.

GETTING SMART

Please come pick me up. I want to go home.

"There must come a time in every mother's life where they need to let their child fly away, even if the child has a broken wing."

It's hard being on your own as you go to so many new places with so many unfamiliar faces. I wish you were here with me.

"You're alone now and with that you need to learn how to make amends."

No mother please don't let me go. I'm frightened, I'm just too weak. Please hold my hand.

"We're always just a phone call away."

It's different. It's too hard for me to even speak about what's bothering me so deeply.

"Maybe you need to see a therapist."

If I can't talk to you then how could I possibly speak with a therapist?

"Well, it beats talking to yourself."

At least when I do that, I know he's listening to me.

"Don't get smart with me."

I didn't mean to. I'm sorry, I'm just very scared!

"The world is a scary place when you choose to walk alone."

I didn't choose this. My situation is completely different.

"How so?"

It's hard to explain.

"As is everything with you, child."

I'm sure you're completely free from blame.

"There you go again getting smart with me."

I can't help it.

"But there are some things you can help."

What does that mean?

"It's open to interpretation."

That just sounds like pure laziness to me.

"If there's one thing I'm not, it's lazy, it's simply not in our genes."

I never said you were lazy. I said your advice was lazy.

"Well, if you want some real advice then all you had to do was say so. If you're so determined to do this on your own or not at all then you better be prepared for your journey into the unknown."

That just sounds even vaguer than the first.

"You'll understand one day soon."

Well, if you say so.

"For the last time I do not want to hear you being smart towards me."

I know. I know. I'm sorry. I have some homework. I need to finish up, but I'll call you in the morning.

"Promise?"

I promise.

"Okay, have a nice night. I love you."

I love you too.

IT COMES WITH NATURE

I'm searching for a quiet place where the voices in my head can't be heard. A solemn and lonely space where my thoughts can be blurred. As I contemplate the things that should not matter, they cause my world to crumble and shatter. So I go on a journey, to a place far away from here in hopes that I may find the peace that I do ever so desire.

I go for a lovely walk out in the country for a sense of purpose. When times are tough for me, I tend to go to nature as my safe place. Not because of anything particularly interesting but rather I find the outdoors and its inhabitants to be rather pleasing.

The sounds of the birds are the loveliest song a person could ever dream of. They are all quite similar, yet they are also unique in their own special way. Sometimes when I come here, I'm graced with an entire chorus of birds putting on a show just for me. However today there is only one bird, standing on a branch ever so scared and alone. He sings his song, nonetheless. "Are you okay, little guy?" I ask the bird. Surprisingly the bird flew right into my hand and upon further inspection I can say with rather certainty that this was a bobwhite. I am quite fond of the bobwhites as they would serenade me and my mother as she would walk to me to school each day. "Listen to that," she'd say. "Isn't it so beautiful?" I would agree with her and smile as we walked together with such a lovely sound.

"Well, hello!" I say to the bobwhite and it can only peck my hand in response to this. Not in a harmful way, it pecks lightly in a way that I can say was similar to a kiss. It seemed to be quite fond of me as I am for it as well. The bird flies away hastily as many birds tend to do, however even though I know this to be a fact it still fills me with immense sorrow. I am alone once again and seeing as I currently had nothing better to do, I decided to follow this beautiful creature.

I head north into the woods and begin my journey. I'm surrounded with beautiful trees on all sides with no sign of a world outside of these trees other than the occasional ray of sunlight that peeks its head through the assortment of leaves. I am in awe of such an image occurring right before me. I dare say that the best description I can give for this gift of God is that it's something that reminds me of a Romantic Era painting.

I continue to walk along the dirt path only to become sidetracked by that mischievous Mother Nature yet again. This time it comes in the form of a lovely formation of rocks that happen to catch my eye. It must have reached at least 10 feet high in total which I felt was just taunting me to try and climb it. So, climb I did, and after a few minutes of struggling to find a good place for my feet, I'm able to scale my way up this stone monument of life.

Once I reach the top, I'm astounded by the sights I see. I feel so tall and mighty as I look down on God's beautiful creations.

It reminds me of one of those "once in a lifetime" experiences I had heard so much about while never seeing one for myself. I can see over the trees to find a whole new world of life and of possibility for myself. I found an amount of amazement in that idea which could be quite similar to that of a child. With the cool breeze flowing through my hair, I am inspired to continue my quest to see what more mysteries are still to be seen in this land of joyous miracles.

Down the dirt path once again to the museum of nature I go. I become fascinated with everything I see around me as I find it difficult to close my eyes for even the slightest second, thinking that I would miss out on another simplistic yet life-changing sight. I hear the crunching of the leaves as I look over at the perfect time to see a fox with its tail in the air running across the free land. To think about how much wildlife call this place their home is truly compelling to me, this is not the sort of question that the general public would ask for they have become too consumed with humanity and their consumerism wants.

Those of us who make up the human race do not care as much about the other life that makes up this planet. A majority of us walk by every day without even proposing a thought or care to the flowers or the trees or even the animals. We are too invested in the media and our own personal lives to care about what was here long before you and me. We try to destroy it all and take advantage of what this world is truly made up of. Both wars and pollution have harmed the world, yet nature lives on regardless of this fact. Nature hurts from this; however nature still has the opportunity to grow and adapt, something

I admire deeply. Even after we're gone the trees and the animals will all still be here and thrive. Unbothered by our absence, they will live their days the same as they always have and always will. This is one of life's many certainties.

I know this and I have accepted this wholeheartedly as I hike along this path made for me. I take in the sounds around me like the wind rustling through the leaves and the rare noises of various animals here and there. Other than that, it is absolutely silent, both physically and mentally. This is what I have searched for - absolute inner peace. I rest my head under the shade of an oakwood and close my eyes knowing that I have found that happy place I needed.

My eyes snap open at a familiar sound. I look up to see a bobwhite perched in the tree above me, singing to its hearts content. I stare in curiosity. Could this be the same bobwhite I had sought after? I listen closely and I recall...Yes! This was definitely the same bird! It flies into my hand once again and I can't help but become overcome with so much glee. This is nature, this is life in its purest form. So, the bobwhite and I shall sit together and sing in harmony for as long as it shall please us.

BE A REAL MAN

"Now boy, always make sure to wear your finest suits on Sunday. There mustn't be any wrinkles in it unless you plan on looking like a fool. The last thing I want someone to think is that I raised my boy to be a laughingstock. Don't chew your gum too loudly around the company you keep. You don't want to be a nuisance who distracts those around him do you? You need to keep up with your studies, I expect nothing less than valedictorian. You better come home with straight A's on your report card. Do well in your studies and you can find yourself with any job you want, well, any job that would take you, that is.

Once you get that good job, you will finally be able to support your future wife and children at home. A real man doesn't make his wife have a job or go to work. So, tell me, are you going to be a real man? Never let anyone see you crying, only boys can cry. Men are supposed to be strong and stoic, yet you still weep like a little child would. It doesn't matter if the other kids call you names or pick on you, you can't give them the glorious satisfaction of seeing you cry.

Eat all the vegetables on your plate. You want to become big and strong like a real man should, just like your old man did. However, you're not like him at all are you? By the looks of it you have not one muscle on your body, and you still call yourself a man? You won't find yourself getting the girls' attention by looking scrawny and pathetic. Do twenty more push-ups right now, because nothing will change with you sitting on your ass all day.

Never back down from a fight that presents itself. Don't even think about giving up or letting the other person pummel you. You're fighting for your family's honor, so you better come out the victor, lest you want your family to be nothing more than the laughingstock of the town.

You need to learn to survive and adapt to this world around you, because the path you're heading on now isn't going to help you at all. In this world, it's either eat or be eaten, so which one will you choose? You can either become a real man or live as the mere boy you seem to be so satisfied in being."

THE FAILED WRITER

The failed writer does not rest at night. He is too busy trying to fill the void that is left from the blank page. No words are destined to appear, for his heart is in the wrong place. He writes out of urgency and the need to finish by a designated date. But dear reader and literary hopeful, this is not the true way of a writer.

Writing is a form of art and therefore should be treated as such. The true writer creates his art not because it is asked of him but because his heart drives him to it. It is the true passion and meaning behind a piece of writing which truly makes it art, which I feel has become lost on many writers of the current era. Let it be noted that I as well fall into this category of the "lost writers" although it angers me so. Unlike many others, I try to improve and become a better writer day in and day out, although unsuccessfully, I must admit.

Think of what the likes of Shakespeare or Wordsworth would feel towards my writing. They would most likely despise it, I assure you. As times change so do our customs and our ideals but what I would do is go back into a time machine to learn from some of the greatest writers of all time. I could shadow the likes of Charles Dickens, Ernest Hemmingway, and perhaps even Mark Twain.

I begin to write some lines, in hopes of finding a good sense of creativity, however my mind has become cluttered, and my writing definitely shows this.

"Though I've tried to face the storm head on,
I lay my head in shame and cry for the battle is done,
I wave my flag with lost pride,
as I stare at the rising sun."

No, no, no, this is all quite ridiculous. What am I trying to convey? What is the message I want to tell? I'm angered at myself for writing such a bland piece of work, in my heart I feel as though I am much more talented than this cluttered mess of words shall lead you to believe. I hang my head in shame as I tear my "masterpiece" into pieces, I can do better than this. No, I *must* do better than this!

"I'm destined to lose, though I tried hard.
The storm is mightier than the sun.
Though I may leave this world soon,
I must keep going for the war has only just begun."

I read these four lines again and think to myself how absolutely dreadful the words are. What's the story? There isn't one, I'm only cursed to write stories from my life, my creativity otherwise is quite drained. If I never allow myself to leave my body as a writer, then my works will most definitely suffer for this. I've attended many writing classes to help me with this, mind you, but it was never to any avail. I read from the works of many great authors, although I could not seem to comprehend them. Instead, I'm in my head trying to conquer the dreaded writer's block. I've tried many ways of preventing this, even going so far as to experiment with different forms of writing. Poetry, novels, even screenplays came and went through my mind leaving nothing of substance for me to work with.

I listen to many of my classmates recite their written work, leaving me both amazed and envious by their writing process. What they write has raw and real emotion. While mine is a mere carbon copy of what I have previously written, unable to write something new. Their stories have meaning while mine are nothing more than a confusing cluster of words and ideas.

Was I truly destined to become a writer like I had originally planned? Or am I merely a fraud in writer's clothing?

I listen to the beautiful words that come out of their mouths, and it makes me weep. For these people who I am surrounded by in class are everything I had planned on being and more. They were scholars and sophisticated as there ever was. I, on the other hand, had come from a life in the country where people did not hold much value in reading and writing. The town's people couldn't care less about your mental ability as long as you were able to work on a farm. I was born quite scrawny and small therefore I was proven to be very useless when it came to my chores.

The kids would laugh at me and say, "There goes Billy again with his head in a book. How about you do something meaningful?" But I was doing something meaningful, that is, it was to me. While the other kids would run around playing tag to pass the time, I was hiding in the barn reading whatever I could get my hands on. The words would fly off the page and

I was taken to a whole new world of imagination and beauty. It was at that moment that I decided to run away from this place I called home for good. There were to be no more friends or family to think of, just myself and the open road with a pencil and notebook in hand.

Should I have left? Looking back on it, it hardly seems like it was worth leaving my life behind. I have written no works that I am proud of, nor have I felt like I learned anything of value. The only thing that I was able to take away from this was that I cannot and should not be a writer; if I were to be, I'm quite sure by now something would have occurred to awaken something in me. However, this never came, and just like a volcano I stayed dormant for years in hopes that one day my creativity would explode.

The class claps for the reader, her poem about the sounds of rain on a cool spring day.

Simplistic in its idea, yes, but its execution was on a whole new level. I want to be like her one day, I tell myself, although I know this will fall upon deaf ears. It has been ten years since I've begun this journey to become a world-renowned writer and I subsequently have failed in every single moment. The reader sits down, and I stare at her in awe. I was in awe at how this complete stranger made a work that would surely impact the way I think for the rest of my life.

I recall another time in my life when I had been struggling. I sat in this cold dark alley that had become my home after I had lost all the money with which I began my journey. Expenses such as food and shelter were always expensive in those days, therefore I feel as though I brought that situation upon myself as I should have been better prepared. I hid under a crate as the rain began to pour down upon me. This would have not been an issue, as I had done this many times before, if not for one slight misstep, I had left my notebook out in the rain all night long.

I woke up in the morning to find all of my writing to be absolutely drenched, destroying any remnants of hope I had of being a writer. I cried for my many, many destroyed works that would never be seen by the human eye ever again. That was the weakest moment in my life and I'm trying to recall what had convinced me to stay on this journey. I believe that it was simply my own fortitude that had pushed me to continue. "Don't stop now, you're halfway there," I'd tell myself as I marched down the city streets hoping to get my big break in the world of literature.

Oh, how naive and ignorant I was back then. If I had known that it would lead to another four years of nothing, then I believe that I would have stopped my journey, given up on my dreams, and gone home. But there's a reason we as humans cannot see the future; that's because it has already been planned out for us and we must follow through with that plan given to us. So yes, I feel like I made the right decision to continue my literary journey, because if I were to tell myself otherwise it may just lead to more disappointment and sorrow, which I already have more than enough of.

"Mr. Adams, could you read us some of your works?" the teacher asks of me.

I stumble upon this question for a moment, being caught off guard, lost in the thought process of my past and present and inevitable future. I'm frozen in fear, my hands and forehead have begun sweating profusely.

What if they hate it? What if they know I'm a fraud? I could never face these scholars again!

"Mr. Adams, could you please come to the front and read some of your literary works for the class?" the teacher asked again, looking a little perplexed by my attitude.

"Yes ma'am, I shall give it my best shot." This was a lie, but I've always been a devout follower of the rule, "fake it till you make it". I stand at the front of the class and see all these pairs of eyes looking and glaring at me from all ends of the room. Why must I put myself through this torture? I clear my throat and in a very feeble and weak voice I recite my poem:

"Though I try to face the storm head on,
I lay my head down and cry.
For then the battle is done,
I'll be the one to wave my flag with lost pride."

After I finish the audience erupts into applause. I'd never received such a warm reception before, especially with my writing. This writing, this poem that I wrote was my most despised piece; it made no sense, I would tell myself. Yet here I stand in front of tens of people who have enjoyed what I had to say, something that I never even experienced in my hometown. I go to my seat with an enormous smile on my face, as I had proven to that classroom and to myself why I'm here. Why I wake up every day and grab a pencil and paper, and I bring my words to life. Because while I may not like it myself, my writing keeps me busy and passionate when I feel most like giving up.

The bell rings and the students all disperse. Except one, the lovely girl from earlier who had written about the spring rains. "I really liked your poem," she said to me.

I smile back at her, saying, "Thanks, I enjoyed yours as well." Thus began what I believe to be my first friendship. The two of us walked out of the classroom together as we discussed our dreams and aspirations for our writing, and more importantly, the world.

HOW I BECAME A PRO WRESTLER

Every Saturday night I would sit with my father as the lights from the television screen lit up our faces. We would see such amazing performers put on a show that I will always fondly remember, with the likes of Jay Lethal, The Briscoes, and Dalton Castle blasting each other with hard hitting moves. Many have claimed that they do not get the appeal of professional wrestling; they say that it is too "fake" for a distinguished mind to be entertained by. After all it is just men in glorified underwear fighting with each other, what's so great about that?

Well, there's so much more to it than that. The overall presentation of flashy outfits and characters is what first caught my attention to the squared circle. Admittedly everyone has their own guilty pleasure that they would never admit to liking, and I feel as though wrestling will forever be mine.

We looked to the television to see an amazing high flying move over the top rope that left my and my father's mouths wide open in shock. It was at this moment that I looked over to my loving father and said, "One day, I'm going to be just like him. I want to be a wrestler."

My father just laughed at this statement, perhaps pleased that his son had acquired such big dreams at a very young age. "You can do anything you set your mind to, son," he said to me with the proudest smile on his face as we continued watching our favorite pastime.

It was a little over one year later when my father finally had the opportunity to take me to my first wrestling show. I was ecstatic to see all of my favorites from the television finally up close and personal. Once we had arrived the atmosphere was mesmerizing. The spotlights shined down on the stage and the ring. Thousands of people with interests just like mine, filling every last remaining seat in the venue. For the next three hours I do not believe I sat down once as I was too caught up in the action and pure spectacle that was in front of me.

We saw body-slams, suplexes, even the occasional top rope elbow! It was truly one of the most amazing experiences of my life as I cheered on my favorite while wearing a tee shirt that my dad purchased for me, although it was two sizes too large. "You'll grow into it," he said. "After all, if you are going to be a wrestler you have to get big and strong!" I thought about this for a moment as I looked at myself in the restroom mirror. I was not like the other athletes at my school, and especially not like the ones I saw in action that night. I was small, both in my weight as well as my height. It was at this moment that I contemplated whether I could ever become a wrestler or if I was just destined to be a fan for the rest of my life.

"Are you okay? You look lost." I look into the mirror to see none other than the body of the world champion, Josh Graham, standing only inches away from me.

I was starstruck, for I had never been within the same building as a famous person, let alone right next to one. "H-- Hello sir, I'm sorry I didn't mean to bother you." I managed to stumble over the words.

"You're not bothering me at all!" he said happily.

"I'm okay, I'm just upset."

"Well, that would mean you're not okay at all."

There's a long pause as I try to talk to one of my life heroes. I had dreamt of this occasion many times before, however, it is quite different in real life, I must admit. "I saw your match tonight. It was the best!" I say to the champion as I try to change the subject.

"Thanks kid," he said with a very polite smile across his face. "I see you're wearing my shirt too," he added.

"Oh yes! I just got it tonight. You're my absolute favorite wrestler!" I begin to ramble, and I look to his face to see him shaking his head in amusement, most likely this was not the first time he had heard such a claim.

"Well kid, maybe one day you can be a wrestler too. Then people will say that you're their favorite wrestler."

I froze as I wondered if I heard him right. "Are you serious?"

"Of course, I'm serious, I don't say these things to every fan I come across, you know."

"But...I'm so small. I could never be like you or the others."

"It's not the size of the fighter, but it's the size of the heart in him."

It was with that statement that I began to have a revelation. Perhaps my dreams could still be accomplished as long as I put in the work to get there. I decided my small size would not hold me down any longer, I was on a mission to prove myself wrong.

"Good luck out there, kid, I hope to be seeing you again someday." Graham told me as he made his exit. It was this completely random meeting that would inspire me for years to come.

I walked back outside to find my father waiting there for me. "Where were you?" he asked worriedly.

"I was learning something important," I answered vaguely.

"Well, you sure missed a lot. The world champion was just here!" He wasn't aware that I already knew this. "He even had time for me to get you this," my father said excitedly as he handed me an autograph.

I stared at it in amazement, the thought of this gift alone was enough to bring me to tears, but it is the words he wrote that made me love it even more.

Dear Austin,

Thanks for your years of support! Remember that no matter if anyone tells you differently, always follow your dreams.

Best wishes, Josh Graham

These are the words that I will continue to live by for the rest of my living days. The words followed me as I trained to become stronger, learning the ways of the ropes. They followed me with every new move I would learn along with every new friend and foe I made along the way. The words were the only thing present in my head during my first match in front of a measly crowd of ten people.

Many professional wrestlers would scoff at the idea of performing in front of ten people, but I truly did not care as long as I was doing what I loved. To make the moment even sweeter one of those ten would be my father, who helped me along my venture into the ring. "I'm so proud of you," he said to me.

"I told you I was going to do it, maybe you should have put more faith in me," I teased him. We embraced each other in a hug that would last close to a minute as we both let each other know how much we loved the other. A moment not made great by the cool moves or characters, but because I had achieved my goal in life and my father, my best friend, was there to witness it firsthand.

I was not the only person wrestling that night. When I looked at the call sheet earlier in the day, I saw none other than Mr. Graham's name listed. I personally made it my duty to find him. This would be my chance to talk to him, so I searched all over the arena. However, I began to fear that he had left. But my fears would soon be put to rest as I turned my head to the locker room door to see Josh Graham in the flesh. Admittedly he looked quite a bit older, as it had been years since our first encounter, but that's the same story with everyone now, isn't it?

Even though he had aged, his enthusiasm didn't seem to have left him as he had the same look on his face that he did all those years ago. "Hey kid, good match out there!" he said to me as he patted me on the back.

"Thanks, sir, it means a lot coming from a legend like yourself." He sat beside me and we talked for hours about numerous things. The life on the road, being away from family, injuring ourselves…all for the amusement of others.

Finally, I asked him, "Say, do you remember me from all those years ago?"

He smirked and said with such honesty in his voice, "I meet a lot of people, care to jog my memory?"

"Well…" I began, "years ago on a fateful evening I had the chance to meet you for the first time and even though I was just a kid you went out of your way to make my day, to make me feel like I existed."

"Well kid, eventually you realize that the fame and the glory that comes with this won't last forever so it's best to make as many memories as you can while you're here."

"Thanks, still wise after all these years I see?" I asked him humorously.

"It's a process. You start off as nothing more than a kid with a dream and you build off of that. As long as you keep working and never give up you can accomplish anything."

After this, I shook my mentor's hand, knowing I had to meet back up with my father towards the front of the venue. "It was a pleasure seeing you again sir." I said to him.

"Same to you kid, and by the way it's not the size of the fighter that matters, it's the size of the heart in him that's important."

I could only smile after hearing his same piece of advice again after all these years. I walked out of the locker room with my head held high above my shoulders, knowing that my heart was more than big enough to make my dream a reality. Without my father or Josh Graham, I don't know where I would be and I'm thankful for that, because as I walked down the hallway, I knew that they helped me become a pro wrestler.

A LOST LOVER'S TRAGEDY

Love. It's quite frankly the loneliest feeling with quite the confusing meaning. I swore I had loved a woman long ago, only to throw all of that away without so much as a second thought as to how it would affect her. I was living a lie because I was dreaming of a much better and happier life than the one I had been dealt by fate's most unforgiving hand.

I had planned this out long in advance and much to her ignorance as she looked at me with her rose-tinted glasses. She was, I believed, happy, and for many months I had tried to convince myself that the feeling was mutual. However, this had only drawn me with more urgency to want to fall off the face of the Earth, just to get away from her. Not because she was particularly awful to be around, but that she was just so bland. While she was one of the most gorgeous people I ever had the privilege to lay my eyes upon, her personality was, for a lack of a better word, abysmal.

It was far too common during our time together that we would run out of things to talk about. This was not for lack of trying, as I would try to chat with the woman about things that interested her, like her favorite genre of book or her taste in music. Once I asked these questions, however, I would discover that she had no such thing! "I like it all equally," she would constantly say.

"Who likes everything? That's absurd, you must have a favorite book or a song that you enjoy!"

But she could only respond, once again, with that awful phrase, "I like it all equally."

One fateful night when we sat next to each other in bed I began to devise my plan to leave her with the least possible amount of harm inflicted on both parties. One last night out on the town, I thought to myself. Then when she least expects anything, I shall make my escape like a criminal on the run. I decided that it would be best to create an alias for myself so that she would never be able to find me. I needed something believable, something that was so ordinary that no one would give a second thought to it. I settled on the name of Tom Jones. After all, were you to meet someone with that name you most certainly would not give a second thought to whether he was telling the truth. It was the safest option.

When the sun rose the next morning, I informed the lady that we would be going to the ballroom that evening. She was overjoyed by the news and immediately went to go find the best dress for the occasion. I, meanwhile, began to feel an amount of guilt for what I was planning to do later that night. I was almost able to talk myself out of completely abandoning the relationship as I knew this would be morally wrong. However, I had already made up my mind. I decided I would live with the weight of this guilt in hopes that I might eventually find my soulmate, someone I could talk to for hours upon end about whatever pleased us that day. I wanted something real.

Love. It will not last for long yet it's the most beautiful song. She took my hand for a dance for what would become one last night of romance. I cannot recall the name of the song. It was a song of her choosing which was not to my particular taste whatsoever. It was slow, so slow that it felt as though the song would never end. My palms were sweaty as my heartbeat rose quite high with nervousness.

She looked me in the eyes and my heart began to feel too much pressure with the situation.

Those were eyes of a pure soul and not one who deserves such torment with their emotions. She was so beautiful in her long pink dress, but beauty can only get a relationship so far. Sure, looks are important to some, but not enough people put a value on the mind behind the beauty. The mind is more beautiful to me than any physical appearance, for at least then I would not be so bored!

As soon as the unbearable song ended, I thanked the woman and excused myself to the restroom. I never went back to get her or even so much as check up on her. Like the awful person I was, I ran away from a situation that I deemed too difficult. By the time she would have realized my exit and most likely begun her mourning, I would have already been too far gone. This is where this story should have ended. But sometimes, the Lord works in mysterious ways when you least expect it.

It was almost twenty years to the day as I recall, and I had long since made my residency somewhere far out by the countryside. I had long since forgotten my guilt from that venture all those years ago as I developed a new life with a nice house and a family to go with it. The woman I had chosen to be my wife was Janine, who was quite fair in her appearance and attitude, to say the very least. We had two girls, aged ten and twelve respectively, who were about as different as two children could be. But they were happy, as was I.

One night during dinner I heard a knock on the door. I went to answer it to find a young man, no more than nineteen years of age, who enquired, "Is there a Mark Mayhew that resides here?"

I looked at him with shock, as no one had called me by my birth name since that night. "I'm sorry, there's no one here that goes by this name. Now if you could please leave me and my family…" I tried to tell the boy, but he pulled out a photograph and handed it to me before I could finish my statement.

"This is you in the photo, correct?" he asked me. I looked at this picture of me in my younger days with a woman.

"Why, yes, I'd say with great certainty that this is me." I declared honestly.

"Do you recall the woman you are with at all?" he enquired.

"Vaguely, yes, I remember her from a long time ago. It must have been about…"

"Twenty years." The young man finished my thought.

"How do you know that?" I asked him curiously.

"Because the woman in that picture is my mother," he revealed to me, much to my shock and dismay.

"I don't know what to say," I honestly said.

"You can start by saying it's nice to meet you, son," he bluntly said.

"Are you sure I am your father?" I asked him, hoping there may have been other possible suitors she had been seeing.

"After you left, she swore off love for the rest of her life. She thought you were her soulmate and the idea of you leaving her was too much to bear. Therefore, she put all of her time and effort into raising me. She even felt inclined to name me after you. She did this because she was so certain that one day you'd come back and we could finally be a big happy family, but that day never came," he said to me quite angrily, and I could not blame him.

I would have been angry too had I never gotten the chance to have a father. It was then that my wife entered the living room, curious as to what was taking me so long to return to our family dinner.

"Hello! Tom, is this a friend of yours?" she asked.

"Oh yes, this is Mark. He was just leaving," I said, as I had been wanting to abruptly end this family reunion since it had started.

"Please Mark, why don't you stay for dinner?" her house host instincts came out.

"Well, Mark is busy, darling. He must return to school in the morning," I said.

The young boy looked at me with such a blank expression that I could not begin to guess as to what emotion he felt in that moment.

"I would really enjoy a good meal before heading back to town," Mark said.

I glared at him with urgency. If looks could speak, mine would have definitely said, "Please don't tell her I had another life." I feared what my wife and children would think of me if they were to know the truth.

"Great. Tom, go grab a seat for our guest!" my wife told me.

"Yes, dear," was all I could reply.

Upon my return with the chair, it was much to my surprise that the young man who claimed to be my son was getting along quite well with my family.

The two girls were unbothered, as they continued to bicker among themselves, although it appeared as though Janine had some interest in Mark. "So, Mark, how do you know Tom?" my wife asked as an excuse for small talk.

"He knows my father," he said rather bluntly.

"What is his name?" my wife questioned.

"Mark."

"Mark? Why that's quite funny. Tom has never mentioned a Mark."

"He began working for us just the other week dear, I could have sworn I told you," I told my wife.

My wife looked skeptically at the both of us. "So, tell me a little bit more about your father, Mark," my wife demanded of our guest.

"Well, I don't really have a good relationship with him, honestly. He is not around very often, you could say, and with my mother passing away last year I feel as though I am alone quite often," Mark said as he stared directly into my eyes.

I knew in that moment that there were a lot of things that this man had never gotten to say to me, and he would not make his exit until he made sure that all of those things were said.

"My condolences, losing a mother can be devastating," Janine said, in an attempt to console him.

"Thank you. There's something I would like to ask, madame. Would it be too much stress on yourself for a glass of water?" Mark said politely.

"Of course! I'll be right back." Janine had gotten up to leave and that was my chance to get rid of him just like I had his mother.

"Is it money you want?"

"No."

"Then why are you here?"

"Because I wanted closure."

"Well, you got it, so please leave."

He looked at me with quite the angry glare as he said, "Closure is more than just seeing your father after twenty long years. There are so many things that I need to say to you before I can say I have closure."

"Goodness, what's with all the ruckus in here while I was gone, boys?" Janine reentered and attempted to dissolve the conversation.

"It's nothing dear. Mark is just a big fan of the Jets, so things just got a little heated," I said, in hopes yet again of concluding the situation.

"Oh yes, Tom watches a lot of baseball, so you two should have a lot to talk about," Janine added.

"You don't say?" asked Mark, knowing this would prolong this awkward dinner even further.

"Yes, dessert should not be too much longer," my wife said as she handed him a glass of water. She left the room once again, leaving me and my son to stare at each other.

"I'd really like you to leave. I'm sure it would be better for both of us."

"Better for the both of us? You've never once thought about what's best for me."

"I didn't know you existed. She never told me about you."

"She was going to inform you on the night you left. Quite the inconvenient timing."

I sat in my chair as the guilt I had received all those years ago had returned.

"I don't want you to be a father to me, quite honestly it is too late for that. I merely came to see what kind of man you were, and I must say, I did not expect much of your character and yet I am still disappointed."

"I am truly sorry. If I had known, I would have been there for you," I said as I tried to console him and ease the tension of the situation.

"Yes, the word "if" truly holds a lot of meaning there, doesn't it? There are no ifs, ands, or buts that can be said with good confidence for me. You had the chance to create for yourself a new life as I see here, much better than the life that had been given to me. You get to rest your head at night without any thoughts as to who you may have wronged on that day. It's plainly obvious to me that you just don't care," Mark said to me.

I reflected upon his words and became filled with so much sadness over how my own flesh and blood could think so little of me. He'd been planning this day for a long time, I could see by the look in his eyes. A look of disgust and hatred, all caused by none other than myself. "I'm quite sorry if you feel as though I have impacted your life so negatively," I said to him.

"I cannot accept your phony apologies. My questions have been answered. I wish you a good day, *father,*" he retorted.

He walked out of the same door he had entered without looking back, just like I had done those years prior to his poor mother. I should have gone after him, but I didn't. I felt as though it would have been better not to. He didn't need a father; he was strong on his own. Being with him would have just made that worse.

My wife came back out a few minutes later, wondering where our prestiged dinner guest had gone. I told her that he had to leave immediately because his father had called him, but I feel as though you could say he was the one that called his father.

"That's a shame. He was such a nice young man. We should have him again sometime," she said. "You know, Mark reminds me of someone I've seen before, I just can't put my finger on it."

A SOCIALLY AWKWARD BOY: THE STAGE PLAY

I had always been quite the loner when it came to school. It was commonplace for me to be nervous about interacting with absolutely everyone. This caused me to stay at the back of the classroom as I hoped to be unnoticed by the masses. I didn't have friends per se, and I doubt very many people knew who I was at all. I was a background character in a world full of Broadway's biggest stars, so it seemed.

I was walking to my classes on what was a very rainy Wednesday morning. I walked past the bulletin board of announcements just like I had done many times before, normally not paying any attention whatsoever to calls for after-school programs and similar organizations. However, this time there was a flier that caught my fancy. "Auditions for the school play: Tuesday at 7." I had never acted a day in my life before yet there was something that drove my heart to want to participate in the show.

My anxiety crept up on me more with each passing day as I got closer to the auditions. My brother, an actor when he was in school, was very talented and I've always had a hint of jealousy towards him because of it. He was able to put himself out there in ways I could not dream of doing, which only drove me to acting even more. Being in college can be quite an experimental time for anyone and I wanted to experiment with how much I could put myself out there without dying of embarrassment.

Tuesday soon came and I had not been able to sleep the whole night prior with the nervousness in my soul about being on stage. Not only in front of hundreds of people, but alongside people that I had believed to be more talented and outgoing than I was. Upon entering the theatre, I was greeted with many perplexed looks. "Who is that guy?" and, "I've never seen him before," were some of the passing remarks, which in turn caused even more anxiety about the event. I am but a stranger to this room full of people who had represented a family.

I sat in the back, hoping to stay unnoticed until it was my time to perform on the stage. Auditions began soon after and I witnessed quite the spectacle in watching these actors. There was a young woman with the most beautiful raven black hair, with an amount of humor in her performances that had left me almost rolling on the floor from laughter. The way she would use her mannerisms while on that stage was amazing, I could hardly look away for a second. Performing alongside her was this very nice looking fellow, with long flowing hair and facial hair that even I was jealous of. The way he talked captivated me so much, I believed for a moment that this man really was the character that he had painted himself to be.

How am I going to do even half as well as that? I asked myself. My heart was racing faster than I had ever remembered. I looked over to see a boy who looked to be about the same age as me.

"First time?" he asked me politely.

"Yes, have I made it that obvious?" I asked him worriedly.

"A little bit, I have to admit. You're not alone though, I've never done this either," he said to comfort me. "I'm Nick, by the way," he said as he extended his hand.

"Will," I responded nervously.

"Well, I wish you the best of luck out there, Will." Nick told me with a generous smile.

"Break a leg," I told him as I got ready to step on the dreaded stage. As I walked to the middle of the stage the lights became ever more blinding to my weak eyes. I took one last deep breath and…

I went through my performance without a hitch but something odd happened. It felt as though it was not me on that stage but someone entirely different that I didn't even know existed. Yes, I stumbled upon my words and sweated profusely throughout the entire scene, but I felt as though that wasn't me. A personality or a version of me? Perhaps, but not the real me.

It helped immensely that I had the opportunity of performing my scene with an experienced actor by the name of Faith, who I felt despite my shortcomings was able to carry me through a halfway decent performance. After we had finished, I became so embarrassed that I had left to hide in the comfort of the men's restroom as I tried to stay unseen by the general public. Many people came and went as I panicked. It felt as though time was destined to stay frozen in that moment.

After somewhere in the vicinity of ten minutes I walked back into the theatre to see my new friend, Nick, in the middle of a scene. I smiled as I found comfort in watching him, he seemed as though he was a natural entertainer, which I felt in that moment I was anything but. I sat with my jaw agape but absolutely and respectfully quiet, for I was having the time of my life as I watched these individuals who were the same age as me, with so much talent and perseverance.

When he was done, he returned to me and asked, "What did you think?"

"Well, I don't think this is your first show, that's for sure," I joked with him.

"I could say the same thing about you," he said with a chuckle.

"What are you talking about? I bombed up there," I said in a not very serious manner, despite the fact that this affected me a great bit.

"You're not giving yourself enough credit. You shouldn't compare yourself to the other people here. They've had a lot more training and work than you but that doesn't mean you're not good. It just means that people like you and I need to work harder and one day, we'll be just like anyone else in here. It all starts when you believe in yourself."

I found this advice to be wise and profound. "And what if they don't like me?" I asked him.

"Then they are missing out on a large amount of potential," he replied.

These words encouraged me to not give up. He drove me to be better in a way I had never conceived of before, by starting with acknowledging my self-worth.

"I have to get going, but I'll see you at callbacks," Nick said to me with a smile. We waved to each other as we went down our separate paths. However, some paths have a knack for intersecting with each other.

Just two days later we met again as we both looked at the call sheet. Despite it being our first attempt at this, we both obtained pretty prominent roles, which left us both in the highest of spirits. Over the next three months the two of us would spend a lot of time together, and soon other people would join our group.

Like Nealy, a beautiful woman with an even more beautiful personality. She is in the Hall of Fame for possessing the kindest and most gentle soul. There were others as well, such as Heidi and Autumn, who would later become like sisters to me just as Nick had become my brother. It's amazing how good relationships find you in the places where you least expect it.

Over the next few months, I would continue to study and improve my skills in the world of acting, all the while developing heartfelt friendships along the way. When it finally came time for the big show, I felt no nerves or anxiety whatsoever. Rather, I felt comfort in going on that stage because I got to have fun with my friends, which was a much sweeter reward than whether I did a good job or not. Those two and a half hours went by so fast that I hardly remembered my cue for curtain call. As I raced out onto the stage for what would be my last time, tears rained down my cheek. Tears of sadness because I had the chance to truly discover who I was and make the best friends I ever had the privilege of meeting, and I was not ready for this experience to be over.

I took my final bow with Nick by my side as the curtains closed on our show and we all went back to our normal lives. Sure, we all grew up and went on to do our own separate things, but I still define these people as my friends. More importantly,

I found every single member of that production to be my newfound family. A family mind you, that chose me just like I chose them. I thank them for that, and I thank my good friend Nick for breaking me out of my isolated shell.

IT CAME FROM THE WHEAT FIELDS

I was always a curious child. I had the tendency to spend all of my free time roaming around the country, mostly to see what kind of trouble I could get myself into. One particular day I came across a field of wheat that had yet to be harvested. The stalks had to be at least double my height as I remember it. This was nothing out of the ordinary as there happened to be wheat fields as far as the eye could see around where I lived. There was nothing but acres of corn, wheat, and other crops that surrounded me. I found this to be absolutely boring. How was a child supposed to entertain himself with nothing but a field of wheat?

I had to use my imagination for amusement and I will honestly tell you as a kid imagination was not a thing I largely possessed. It has only been in more recent years that I have begun to open my way of thinking towards the imaginary. Yet, I was determined to find some fun so I decided that I would walk through this field as if it were a corn maze you would find at a pumpkin patch.

I wandered through the crops, at first not paying any attention to the things that were around me. However, the farther I journeyed into the tall stalks, the more I began to feel scared. I was scared because I had become lost in this strange world, one in which I could not see or feel what was in front of me as I was surrounded by a forest of bland and somewhat dead crops. I wandered for hours as I strayed farther and farther away from my home and any signs of familiarity.

I took one too many wrong turns and it felt as though I was at a crossroads with no idea of where to go. I was just like a lost soul wandering through the afterlife in hopes of finding an eternal home, however I felt as though I was lost and would very well remain so until I would die trapped in this field of broken dreams and mystery. I was too small to make such a big decision about which way I should go next, when I suddenly realized that I was not alone in this field as I began to hear the rustling of the crops against each other like someone or something was heading towards me at a fast speed.

My heart began to race as I began to run aimlessly through the field in hopes of getting away from whatever horrifying thing was present with me in that moment. As the sun began to fall into the night I ran for my life, feeling as though the monster pursuing me would only get closer and stronger as it got nearer to me. I could feel the tears running down my cheek as my screams grew louder with horror.

Finally, it had come to the point where I could not run any farther because my legs had given out from fatigue. I hoped and I prayed that this would be enough for me to lose this monster, yet I heard the rustling some more which led me to believe that it was still on the hunt for me, and it would not stop until that hunger was satisfied. I covered my face with my hands as the rustling became closer as I did not want to lay my eyes on such a scary being. I was crying so much in that moment that I could barely hear the sounds of the beast approaching, yet I knew those sounds were still present.

I held my breath as this terrifying creature showed itself, and as I opened my eyes I could only laugh. This was no monster at all, it was just a kitten! The kitten was one of the cutest creatures I had ever seen in this life. I picked the little kitten up and placed him inside my hand as I began to console it. "Are you lost too?" I asked the feline and it responded with the faintest "meow" which assured me that this animal was not in the best condition. It was small with many of its bones showing, indicating how close to starvation the animal was. I also noticed that this cat appeared to be in quite a lot of pain as it looked like it had been walking around with possibly a sprained leg.

"How could this poor kitten have found its way here?" I asked myself. While I wanted to believe that the cat had merely wandered into this field just like I had, it seemed much more likely that the kitten had been abandoned like many other poor animals in the country, destined to be unloved and unappreciated. There was no possible scenario in which I had left the kitten there, as I felt it would have been quite immoral to do so. So as the young animal sat in my hand, we journeyed through the fields together as we now had companionship to get us to the light at the end of the metaphorical tunnel. The darkness and mystery that had originally scared me so was now my driving force to escape because I now had another life counting on me.

We traveled through the unknown until after seemingly an eternity of walking we finally found the exit the both of us had so desperately desired. When we arrived home, I was scolded by my parents for missing dinner as they were understandably quite worried, until I showed them what I found that day. They were just as astounded by the little creature as I was, so much so that they allowed me to keep him. I would end up naming him "Wheaty" after the chance encounter in which I had found him and Wheaty would quickly become my best friend.

We would constantly play together in the outdoors, even on occasion returning to the wheat field where we had originally found each other. What made this relationship between the two of us so special was not only because he was my first pet, but in a way, my first friend as well. With Wheaty I was given a chance to see the beauty in the animals that keep us company in life because in many ways they are just as lost as we humans are. While Wheaty may have grown since that fateful day, I'll always see him as that scared little kitten who gave a scared little boy hope.

VOICES

"The voices in your head can become the loudest of them all as it feels like you hit one big wall. Blocking you from your beloved family and peers just so they can make sure that you hear them loud and clear. The voices are quite hurtful, and I believe quite rarely sincere, as I weep at the voices that have become too tragic to hear even from my own thoughts and words.

The voices can stop you in your tracks as you're stuck on the way to your final destination. They'll tell you, "You can't do this or that." However, this could not be further from the truth about who you really are. Let it be known that you are nothing less than the brightest shining star on an otherwise dark night. Have confidence in yourself and who you really are because those voices don't know you, only you do. You hold the keys to your success in the palm of your hands if you can just quiet those ignorant and awful voices that are truly not the thoughts of yourself, or anyone for that matter.

As long as you can stay true to yourself and never let go of your beliefs, your goals can surely be achieved. You have the power in your hands to shut those voices out, the voices that represent self-loathing and doubt. You're stronger than them, you're louder than them, and this has become just another hurdle for you to cross! Once you do this it becomes quite plain to see that you have the potential to be your own best friend, but also your worst enemy. This, while one of life's greatest secrets, is also its greatest and most true meaning.

RAINY DAYS ARE FOR THE MEEK

Rain, rain, go away, leave me alone so I may have a good day. Rain keeps falling and I can't feel the sunshine. It has become quite cloudy in my mind, but this has become second nature so it's not too much of a bother. I search for a hint of sunshine as I'm tired of the grey, so I hope and pray that perhaps it will go away, off to another place more needing and deserving of the rain.

It only gets darker as the rain gets heavier. I can hear the harsh pitter patter of the rain as it hits my roof. While some may find the sound to be quite relaxing, I find it rather obnoxious as I know that this will leave me trapped inside for the foreseeable future, which I find unacceptable. I try to write my troubles in the form of poetry to pass the time, but I can only think of those dreaded raindrops, therefore my writing does not consist of anything more than just, "Pitter patter, rain doesn't matter." Which I tear to pieces in disgust and anger.

"Come on, write about anything but the rain," I tell myself as I try again, but the rain becomes louder, though I'm convinced this is just to spite me. How can so many find beauty or calmness in the rain when all it brings is gloominess and despair? Do they not see what I see? I try to write again, only this time to be startled by the sounds of thunder which cause me to finally get up from my desk. "Why must you torment me so, Mother Nature? There's only so much noise a writer can take!" I yell out loud to no one except my cat, who glares at me with befuddlement. He jumps up onto the windowsill to look at all the rain falling and the lightning flashing.

He sits there, not making any noise, just looking at the utter gloominess with amazement, almost as if he finds comfort in watching the wind blow the leaves and the rain droplets all around. I watch him a little longer to see if he will move again but he stands unfazed, almost mesmerized by the utter boringness in the sights. I envy him in a way, my cat is able to find anything entertaining while I can barely focus on what to write about.

I go back to my writing once again:

"Rain keeps falling,
I can't feel the sunshine,
it's so cloudy all the time
and it's making me lose my mind.
Where went the sunshine?
I guess it's not the right time."

I look at the paper with great interest. Perhaps this could be beautiful, I thought to myself. Yet the sounds of the outside world tear into my mind again as I lose myself in this bland and generic writing. Not that I mean to do this, but I just can't let myself freely think in a natural world filled with loud and obnoxious noises that are the rain falling and the thunder. I slam my first against the table in frustration because I know that my mind has become far too cluttered to write or even begin to attempt doing so.

I look back into the living room to still see my cat staring out the window with curiosity. I wish I knew what goes through an animal's brain on a daily basis. Probably not much, I thought to myself as I continued along my journey to find some entertainment on a dreary day such as this. What is so amazing about looking at the rain? It just depresses me. It makes me feel alone and helpless. My cat walks to the door and we both walk outside to sit on the patio together, away from the cold droplets that would inevitably come right at us.

I see my cat running around without a care in the world, ignorant to any troubles. Even in the darkest and coldest of days, he is still able to find his own sunshine. It is at this moment that I have an epiphany. Animals are not simple minded because they could find enjoyment in anything; I was simple-minded because I could *not* find joy in something, and that was Mother Nature. For I failed to realize that any day can be just as beautiful as the next day and only the outlook that someone has can truly make it a "good" or a "bad" day.

Therefore, I walk out into the cold spring rain with my cat and find the atmosphere to be absolutely mesmerizing. The cool wind that rapidly blows through my hair, the raindrops that ever so slightly touch my skin as they fall, and even the dirty mud puddles that my cat makes it his mission to drink out of. It's as if the whole world around us is at peace with itself. This gives me the inspiration to go back inside and try to create something beautiful with my words just one more time. I write and I write some more, all the while not paying attention to the noisy sounds of rain dropping on the roof, or the sounds of my cat shaking all of the water off of him as if he was a heathen. It did not matter as I find myself on a roll, riding on the train of inspiration. Hours later I find myself with a work that is truly full of enlightenment. This only comes in the form of four lines, but they are the four lines that I am most proud of in my entire career and life.

"Rain keeps falling,
yet the sunshine will soon come again.
The clouds will go away once you find your calling.
That's all the knowledge there is to gain."

Simplistic in nature, of course it is. But I feel as though there can also be a metaphorical meaning to it. The rain only comes on the days when you're most weak, but in time those rainy and cloudy days go away the more you find true happiness. I found mine at the behest of a feline who was determined to find joy in life's darkest days. You may find yours anywhere you seek, if you just open your eyes and your heart. I close my book and head off to bed where my cat is waiting for me. Another thing rainy days are good for? Naps. So, we shall now sleep the day away knowing that we both found fun in the rain and the sunshine will greet us shortly.

THE COLORS THAT MAKE UP OUR WORLD

I turn on the television every morning and I'm filled with sorrow and remorse. Not for something that I had done myself but for what my country, my people, have done to this once wonderful place to live. We Americans have claimed to be each other's brothers and sisters, but I feel as though in most recent years we have strayed away from this ideology. Most people are quite colorblind - it's either black and white, red and blue, but no one ever sees the shades of grey that make up our society on an everyday basis.

No one really stops to consider that we need both the red and blue and the black and white in our lives as this gives us a happy medium. No one looks or thinks the same as another so as a country we should acknowledge this and accept this. Instead, there is plenty of ostracization between my fellow countrymen as they either lean one way or the other and you can't choose both. When we should come together hand in hand we instead are greeted with riots, shootings, and more destruction that plague the news I watch every morning. This is because we cannot agree with each other, we've made one another our own worst enemy.

Our ancestors would probably find irony in these events, having dealt with many of the same situations themselves in the era of the Civil War and the Civil Rights Movement, which had been believed to shape our country for the better. However, it appears as though the history of this country is being forgotten, which in turn shall cause it to repeat itself for the rest of time. If we can't come together and learn to accept one another for who we choose to be then we are failing God's declaration of loving thy neighbor as we love ourselves.

I'm only a young man barely out of my teenage years but this scares me because I do not know what the future will hold for us. If we do not start seeing the grey in our everyday life, which is the one true color, then we may never see the bright sunshine rising on a new day ever again. So, grab the hands of your brothers and your sisters America, and do not let go. It is a very bumpy road ahead, but we still have the chance to rebuild ourselves. I turn off the television and I head outside knowing that I've seen all there is for me to see, and now it's time for me to go out and make a change for myself with the help of you and the whole world. Our voices shall be heard as we spread peace and love, with empathy and understanding for the rest of our days.

THE PHANTOM HITCHHIKER

I was driving on this lonely road with no signs of life in sight. I had decided to travel to Florida so I could visit my grandmother. But why drive to Florida when you live in New York? you may ask, and you would be correct! It would have been much easier to have boarded a plane and arrive hours later, whereas by car my GPS had told me it would take days to complete this journey. So why go through all this extra trouble? Because I am deathly terrified of airplanes and the absolutely dreadful heights that they take you to.

I had been on a plane only once in my life, and like a coward I had gotten off before the plane ever took off. I promised myself on that day that I would never so much as step inside of an airport again as long as I lived. So, I drove on this deserted road, only miles into my road trip, and I played some music to ease the eerie quietness that surrounded me. "This has to be the best option," I told myself as I could feel goosebumps crawling down my neck and into my spine. It may take longer, but driving is the safest option. At least this way I am on the ground and in control.

The darkness of the night made it difficult for me to see. However, I did notice one peculiar thing in front of me. In the middle of this dark and deserted road, that looked like it had not been driven on in years, was a man. He was fairly well dressed, with a nice button-up suit and a matching hat to go with it. I slowed down to get a better look at this man. He was without a doubt in my mind the only person I had come across since I turned down this road. This was no short road, mind you. It stretched for miles, and at that point there was no real option for me to turn around on this one-way road, so I drove forward with caution.

The closer I got to the mysterious man the more I noticed what an awful condition his suit was in. It was dirtied beyond belief and looked like it had not been washed in years, along with numerous rips and tears throughout the seams that made me wonder why he had not just thrown the suit out, as it was not fit for living conditions. In his right hand he held a suitcase, which led me to suspect that he was a businessman, or more appropriately judging by his suit, a former businessman.

The car slowed to a halt as I stopped by the man, in hopes of offering him a ride or at the very least, learn more about this strange, strange man. I rolled down my window as the man stared at me unnervingly with his dead eyes. "Where are you heading?" I asked the man. There was no response. "If you're needing a ride, I can take you a little down the road," I offered him. Still no response. His eyes never strayed away from me once, leaving me bewildered. "Suit yourself, old man," I said as I drove off, leaving the old man in the dust behind me.

While I do acknowledge that this incident was odd, I believed the incident to have passed once I had left the man, therefore I continued on my journey which had already proven to be eventful to say the very least. I struggled to keep my eyes open along this boring and never-ending road, but I kept driving as I couldn't imagine anyone in their right mind parking their car in the middle of nowhere so they could sleep. Especially after the creepy incident from earlier I was not taking any chances so I decided to pull an all-nighter until I could find some appropriate shelter.

It was then, to my amazement, I saw the old man from earlier. He appeared once again ahead of me. I was perplexed by this, as I had passed him long ago, only to find him in front of my path once again. There was something odd about the man before, but now I felt that it may have been a case of something supernatural. As I got closer, I was sure that this was the same man! That pale and ghost-like face, his cold and blank stare in those dead eyes. Instead of stopping this time I decided to drive faster, and I soon flew by the man with as much speed as I could pick up.

I looked out my rearview mirror and to my absolute amazement he stood there, unfazed! His stare was still directed at me and me alone; it felt as though he was trying to see directly into my soul. The man just kept aimlessly walking along the road, like he had somewhere to be, but he just couldn't figure out where. As I drove past this unnatural event, my fear began to grow even more. I began to question whether it was just my lack of sleep that had driven me to see this vision. I turned this over in my mind as I hopped between the supernatural and the imaginative, never deciding which one might be the true reason behind this odd man.

I became distracted from the road ahead of me, which was not too much of a danger as the only people I believed to be within a hundred miles were myself and the old man who followed me along my trip. I could feel my hands shake as they tried to hold the steering wheel in a straight and orderly manner. I looked at the sign ahead of me which said, "Gas Station: Next 10 Miles." Thank God, I thought to myself as I saw my almost empty tank. I hoped that my crazy night would soon be coming to its close.

I pulled into the gas station and began pumping up my car. It did not really surprise me that there were no other people present, not even an employee. This place was, I could see, a ghost town. I whistled a tune to keep myself company, and to my surprise someone joined in from the shadows. I listened to the visitor's tune, and it was truly impressive. "I like your tune!" I shouted into the darkness and out of it came the old man once again, to my amazement.

I ran to my car in a mad haste as this man brought so much fear out of me in ways I had not felt before. I attempted to start my car, to no avail. The man crept closer to me which caused even more panic inside me. "Come on, come on!" I yelled as I turned the ignition over and over again, but the car would not start. I began to recite the Lord's prayer as the man stood right in front of my vehicle and I thought in that moment that I was to die at the hands of this man.

The man knocked on my window and my heart practically beat itself out of my chest. I attempted to turn the key one last time and to my relief it worked! I hit the gas as hard as I could in an attempt to escape, and in my haste, fear and panic, I ran over the old man. I looked out the car window to see his body laying motionless on the asphalt. Yet I didn't stop to check on him, but instead ran away from the crime. I'm a monster, I told myself, thinking I had just killed a man, as I drove off into the dark night.

It was soon after this that I passed another road sign. "Gas Station: Next 10 Miles." I could not help but find it odd that there would be two gas stations so close together when we were out in the middle of nowhere. I decided that I would stop anyways to notify my grandmother of my progress. I turned off the road and into the parking lot for the gas station. I dialed my phone only to discover that I had no signal. I stepped outside of my vehicle and walked around in hopes that this would at least obtain me one bar.

To my displeasure I was unsuccessful, and I stared at my phone angrily. I decided to look inside the store, wondering if perhaps there was an attendant who could let me use the store phone. I pulled at the doors only to find that they were locked, meaning I was out of luck once again. As I turned back around, I saw something truly horrifying. It was the old man!

I tried to shout something, but in that moment, I could not utter the slightest sound, I only had the instinct to run, and run I did. I bolted to my vehicle as fast as I possibly could. I looked over my shoulder to see the man charging at me in a mad haste. I reached the car just in time to save myself. As I positioned myself in the car, I noticed that he stood frozen, only feet from the car as he once again stared at me with his expressionless eyes.

"What's your problem?" I finally shouted. I do not know what I was expecting to happen as he just stared at me, unresponsive to my question. I started my car and when I looked back, I could not see him. At this point I did not question the uncanniness of the situation because I had by now become accustomed to being haunted by this man.

I continued on the road again as I rushed out of the gas station. I was relieved and I had hoped that this would be the end of my encounter with this entity. But it was just then I thought that I heard the sound of whistling. It sounded like the same tune I had whistled earlier as I was pumping gas. I turned my head around to see the old man in the back seat of my car with his arms crossed and his signature stare. I screamed with fright as the man grabbed at me. I pulled myself away which inevitably led to me turning the steering wheel so abruptly that I rolled the car over.

We crashed into the ground with such force that I suffered severe whiplash. I struggled for breath as I attempted to escape through the driver side window, but it had become so caved in that I could not even shove my hand through it. Thankfully, I managed to crawl through the passenger side window. I stumbled to my feet as I took in the destruction around me. Upon seeing that the man was still, I began to run, trying my best to wake up from this never-ending nightmare.

After what felt like miles I finally fell to my knees from exhaustion. I could not continue to run away from this man, or anything for that matter. I rested near the side of the road knowing that there would be no cars coming or going. I reached for my phone one more time only to find that there still was no service anywhere near this area. In that moment I felt quite hopeless, unsure of where I was or what was to come.

I lay there with my eyes closed, feeling in that moment as though I had given up on everything, including life. This confusing reality that I had found myself in could not be my own, I was sure of this. I opened my eyes and looked up to see the old man standing in front of me, however, this time I struggled to even gain the energy to get to my feet. "What do you want with me?" I asked.

"I'm here to take you to your destination," he said rather vaguely.

"My grandmother's house?" I asked, confused.

He merely snickered at me in response to this. "You're not going to Grandma's house anytime soon."

"What do you mean by that?"

"Do you know where we are?"

"No." I answered him. "But it looks as though I'm pretty far away from home."

"Home…this is your home now, and it will be for the rest of time," the man said to me.

"But where is home?" I asked him as I motioned to the nothingness that surrounded the two of us.

"Some people call it the crossroads, the passageway from their world to ours. This is death, this is nothingness. This is our end, dear friend." he told me.

"What do you mean this is death? I still feel the same as I ever have! I would know if I had died," I attempted to explain.

"My apologies for neglecting to tell you earlier. This job is always quite hard, however what you say is not always true, sometimes death is something spontaneous, and you don't get the opportunity to feel any pain whatsoever."

"Well, if you're so smart about this, then how did I die?" I asked him sarcastically.

"I do not know; those things are outside of my knowledge and control. I'm merely a chauffeur, if you will, I take the lost souls to their final destination."

"So, I am dead...." I wept as I came to this sad realization.

"Do not cry, there's still so much beauty for you to see," the man said to try and console me.

"But what of my friends and family?" I asked him with concern.

"You will have the opportunity to see them again someday. Believe me when I say, good sir, that this is not the end of your journey. It is merely the next chapter in your existence."

"How much longer until we make it to the end of the road?" I asked with impatience.

"Not much longer, trust me when I say that this will be worth it. Shall we get started then?"

"Indeed," I answered him, as we went back onto that fateful road and walked side by side until we made our way to the glorious afterlife.

Happy Birthday

When I turned eighteen, I decided that I would throw myself a birthday party with all my friends to celebrate a once in a lifetime occasion. I gave invitations to anyone I would come across even if I didn't necessarily know them, as they always say the more the merrier, right? As the day got closer and closer, my excitement could not be contained. It had always been a dream of mine to have a birthday party, however, I was never given the opportunity. Therefore, I decided that I would organize a party entirely for myself.

As the 22nd of May came, I was looking forward all day to seeing my friends and making new memories with them all. I arrived at the destination around six in the evening, which gave me precisely one hour until the party would begin! I hung decorations from the walls and blew up as many balloons as my asthma would allow. I looked at the clock in anticipation as the hour hand slowly made its way to the seven.

Once it had turned seven o'clock, I waited anxiously for my guests to show. Then before I knew it, it was 7:15...Then it was 7:30. Impossible, I thought to myself. "Why would my friends not come to see me on my important day?" As soon as I had asked this, I heard a knock on the door. Upon inspection I could see that this was my friend Nathan who had some of the same classes I did. "Happy birthday," he said with a smile as I welcomed him in and we awaited the start of the party.

"Where is everyone?" he asked curiously.

"I don't know, they should have been here a while ago," I said with utter despair and gloom in my heart.

"I'm sorry," he said. "But just because there's two of us doesn't mean there can't be a party," he said as he patted me on the back.

"Well, what do we do?" I asked him.

"It's your birthday, you can do whatever you want!" Nathan exclaimed. While there was still sadness over being stood up by so many of my friends, I smiled at the idea of doing whatever I wanted on that day.

For that night, neither of us had a care in the entire world. Even though I had felt so alone prior to this, even having just one person to celebrate with was a welcome change. We played video games, watched funny videos, anything that our hearts desired. It had reached the early hours of the morning before we had decided to call it a day. "Thank you for coming, you don't know how much this meant to me," I told him.

He looked around the otherwise empty room for a moment before he told me, "I wouldn't want to be anywhere else." It was on that day that I found a new best friend, or more likely, perhaps he found me. Either way that night taught me the life lesson of "quality over quantity". While it was just the two of us, I believe to this day that the party with just the two of us would have been better than a party with hundreds of us because at least with me and Nathan, we had a memorable evening in more ways than just one.

Every year on our birthdays, ever since that day, we try to see each other just so we can recreate the magic that we experienced on that night. If I could trade that man for all the friends in the world, I absolutely would not do it, because sometimes one person can impact your life in such a profound way that you know they care about you. I know he cared about me on that night when no one else did and for that I have come to appreciate this and accept that my eighteenth birthday, while not as I had envisioned, was without a doubt my most meaningful birthday.

ISOLATION

March 13, 2020. A date engraved in my mind for various reasons. The day that life as I knew it would change drastically. It was just like any other day; I came home as gleeful as I could possibly be due to the coming of the warm spring weather. I had countless hopes and dreams that I planned to conquer that year. I was going to graduate from college, perhaps what would have been the proudest moment of my young life. I had friends who loved and appreciated me, who I made countless memories with, and I had hoped that there would be countless more to come. But oh, how times change!

It was just supposed to be "two weeks to flatten the curve" as I sat at home in fear and confusion over what was going on with the world. The weeks went by rather slowly as I tried to find a way to distract my mind from the harsh reality that had reared its ugly head. I asked myself every month just how much longer I would be locked inside for my own good. As I missed important events like my graduation, Easter, and my birthday, which were usually such happy times for me, however, I felt no enjoyment in these experiences. I still sat at home doing nothing. What was there to celebrate?

I turned to writing in this time of uncertainty. As I could not talk to anyone else, I therefore decided to find comfort in my own words. I wrote until my hands felt as if they were going to fall off and then I would write some more. For time had all but ceased to exist when there was nothing to do and no place to go, so I had more time than I ever knew what to possibly do with. I would write my lines of poetry in disappointment because I could not find the words to properly air my frustrations.

I was mad. I was mad at how people in power could do so little when we needed them most. So many family members and friends who suffered from this virus, some would never recover. There was nothing I could do about it except sit from the comfort of my own home and offer my condolences. So much weight falls onto one's shoulders when there's so much you want to do but no way of doing it. I was locked in this metaphorical prison cell not only physically but mentally as well. After a few months of the same boring routine, I began to lose myself, I was miserable. I found no reason to get up in the morning. There was no reason for me to smile at all.

One year later and the world has begun its routine of healing. I, however, am not healed for the most part. I still deal with these feelings of sadness because I will never make up the lost time or the memories I would have made. I still deal with the fact that I will never get to see my great aunt again because of this virus that took her life. Most importantly, I deal with the befuddlement that some people won't learn from this lesson of a worldwide shut down. They will continue their lives maskless and proud and while that is their right, I feel as though they have missed a greater point. It's not about just one person, it is about every single person around the world. The ones who have suffered and been impacted by the virus are too large to ignore and yet some people still choose to.

Over 31 million people have been afflicted with the virus and yet people still think that this will never affect them. It's sad because that means we are inevitably destined to repeat history once again. This may not happen for many years, but I feel as though we should always keep this possibility in our minds. I pray that the trail of depressing events due to this virus may end soon for the benefit of myself and the world as a whole.

While angry at what has occurred, I must also say that I am thankful for this situation because it has allowed me to grow and to learn. I started quarantine just a scared individual but when it ended, I came out a smarter and stronger person because of it. Without a doubt those 365 days will live in infamy in my mind, but I should also be grateful for the opportunity to pursue my dream as a writer, and more importantly, to become a better person.

March 13, 2020. The day I died, but the day I would forever become reborn in my own image.

THE UNADDRESSED LETTERS

Received January 12th
Dear My Beloved,

I miss you more with each passing day. It feels as if this war will never end as the days progress and more of our men go to the hospital, never to return to the battlefield. I like to tell myself that they have been discharged, although deep down in my heart I know the truth behind what happened to those men and I'm worse off for that. It's hard to close my eyes at night with the faint sounds of gunfire and the screams of those poor men who, like me, were forced to become a part of this battle. I question what has driven us to such extremes as to destroy one another. Are we not all creatures of God? I wish I knew the answer to this. As I put on my clothes every morning and I grab my gun I ponder whether I should just give up now and save myself from whatever amount of trauma I have yet to endure.

Love,
R.W.

Received January 17th
Dear My Beloved.

Not much has changed since the last time I wrote to you. I constantly catch myself dreaming of much simpler times when I was back at home. I think of the lovely walks we would take through the countryside along with the times that you and I would stare up at the stars and tell our deepest wished to each other. Instead, I am thousands of miles away from what made me happy, for "the good of our country", but I do not know what that means. In better news, I have made a friend since I've been here. His name is Jack and even though we are in such gloomy circumstances his spirits still appear to be as bright as they ever were. I envy him for that in a way, but I digress. Jack and I fought tougher for quite a while now and I have never once seen him so much as break a sweat on the battlefield. He also showed compassion to not only me and his fellow soldiers but to the enemy as well. The other day, we passed a wounded soldiers on our way back to base. Instead of finishing him off as we had been taught to do, Jack simply helped the man with what he needed. He gave him his remaining water along with some of the clothes on his back before sending him off. I was amazed by this amount of compassion that he possessed in that moment, it made me gain a newfound respect for him. He is without a doubt the greatest soldier I have seen here during my short period of time at war.

Sincerely yours,
R.W.

Received January 21st

Dear My Beloved,

It appears that I have fallen on hard times. The day started out as normal as any other as we began to storm the enemy base. Jack and myself were walking together and I asked him if he was nervous. To my amazement he said, "No, Robert, I'm not scared. I have all the faith in the world that this war will be over in no time and then we can walk back home proudly waving Old Glory!" I had expected him to at least feel some sense of fear for what we were about to do but he had none. "People like you and me, Robert, we're fighters. There's no way this will be the end of us." I couldn't understand it, but I actually believed what Jack was telling me.

We were going to be alright is what I told myself. The closer we were to the base the more you could feel the stillness in the air. It was like something wrong was going to happen at any given moment, my senses made me sure of this. But as we looked around, we did not see anyone.

Perhaps Jack noticed my discomfort as he said, "Relax, I've got your back." The only trouble was I did not have Jack's back like I thought I had. Before we knew it countless soldiers had jumped out from hiding to reveal themselves to us. Without hesitation they shot at me with their bullets. I had thought in that moment that I was to perish for sure, however it appears as though fate had a different plan for me. Jack pushed me to the ground and covered me as a true hero would have done. I hid under my friend in sheer horror as I could hear the bullet piercing his skin, but he did not utter a sound once. He fell to the ground in pain, and I noticed that he did not have that much longer left to live. I could hear the shouts of "Retreat!" as my fellow soldiers ran without being told twice. As they left, I looked at Jack, who lay still on the ground with the most painful look that I have ever seen. I helped him to his feet and walked with him to base. Once we arrived, Jack was sent to the hospital, leaving me without a friend in this cruel battle. I hope to be the bearer of better news soon, my darling.

Love,
R.W.

Received January 24th
Dear My Beloved,

Jack has taken a turn for the worse. They allow me to see him for a few hours a day, but this doesn't help much as he has fallen into a comatose state. Still, I sit next to him every day and tell him about what is on my mind. I tell him how thankful I am to have met him, I tell him how I had become scared and alone upon being sent here until I had befriended him. He truly makes me feel as though I am valued and when I had the chance to pay him back, I can't help but feel that I failed him. I don't know why he covered me, and I fear as though I may never get the chance to know, but because of it I get to live while the better man pays the price up for it. Yesterday I held his hand and said my goodbyes as I was called for the next mission. This would be the last time I saw Jack as I came back in the morning to an empty room. The nurse kindly told me that Jackie passed away last night in his sleep. I broke down into tears as the nurse embraced me and a hug, as she realized I had not only lost a brother in arms. But also, a friend. His choice to save me will not be forgotten. He truly encapsulated what a hero is, not just a big tough man who could hold a gun. But a man who was kind and compassionate, who cared about everyone he came across. That to me is what a hero is, and Jack was mine. Therefore, I am inspired to go back out in the battlefield and spread the same compassion and kindness that Jack had. If all soldiers here could be just like Jack, then I feel as though we could win this war easily. Not with violence, no, that just makes it worse. We must all use our God given heart to end this violence and destruction.

Love,
R. W.

This was the last of the letters to be found in the remains of EU S Army base.

THE ANGEL WITH BURNED WINGS IS WAVING YOU ON HOME

The demons in my head are quite well and alive. They have slowly but surely taken over every aspect of my life. I can hear and feel them, However, how could I defeat them? It does not matter how fast I run because I can still see. I'm running close behind me. Leave me alone. Please. Just let me live my life.

I feel in my heart are those of sorrow and pain. I just wish everything would stay the same, I just wish my problems would all fade away. I'm surrounded by the shadows in my mind with no light around me to see. When I become surrounded by my demons, they take control over me. As I fell to find an escape, the demons become filled with ecstasy.

I don't need to hear you say I'm not good enough because I tell myself that every day. It has become like a routine for me as it becomes more of a chore. Just a smile. I've been stuck inside my own mind for far too long period like a black hole that just engulfs its surroundings, leaving them to dwell in nothingness for the rest of time.

I can feel my heart piercing through my skin as the demons let themselves in. They mock me and criticize me but most importantly they have allowed me to become distilled from reality. I'm trapped inside my body like a prisoner at war. That is, a war that is waged within myself. With all of my might I climb to the heavens above, only to be dragged back to the hell below. Here I shall stay for all eternity, here it is I have become destined to dwell.

THE MYSTERY BEHIND THE SEVEN SEAS

We made it our destiny to sail the Seven Seas in hopes of finding the mysteries of life that are contained within it. We were a crew of small size, but we had the heart and determination that would allow us to work as well as a crew of one hundred men. I felt the wind flow through my hair as I looked out at the gorgeous sea in front of me. What first had started out as a dream for myself was now my reality.

Admittedly, neither I nor anyone else present on my crew had sailed before so we were all looking to get our sea legs. The five of us had been ridiculed and quite frankly blackballed from ever attempting to sail across the ocean. Therefore, this mission that I had planned for us was to prove to not only the other sailors but to myself that we were destined for greatness.

"Captain, shouldn't we have brought some men with more experience to help us?" I heard one of my crewmates ask me.

"Nonsense! We have brought all that is needed to help us on our journey!" I responded to him rather coldly. He looked at me with a fake sense of happiness, I knew he was worried about our journey, and I was too. Unlike everyone else, I did not have the luxury of showing it. I was their captain and therefore I had to be strong and confident for them.

That night I found myself having trouble falling asleep. I was worried about not only my own life, but the lives my crewmates as well. Nightmares would come and pass that left the strange thought in my mind that the five of us were in major danger. While I wrote this in my journal, I failed to tell the crew for fear that I would cause much unneeded panic. So, I continued as I normally had, keeping these secrets to myself for the greater good of all of us.

When I awoke the next morning, I saw that the sun had failed to rise. It was hidden behind the darkest clouds I had ever seen, making me sure that there would be a storm coming soon. "Captain, it looks very dangerous ahead of us. I feel as though we should turn back immediately!" I heard my first mate try to plead logic into me.

However, this was ineffective as I told him, "We shall sail these seas if our lives depend on it!"

"Yes, Captain," he said doubtfully as he walked down to the deck to help the other crew members steer us through this ungodly storm.

The rain grew harsher the further we progressed, and my heart became filled with more regret in the process. I had the option to give up and make sure these men would live another day, but I had become too invested in this idea of the fame and glory that we would get upon finishing our trip across the seas. My egocentric smile fell across my face as I looked at the dark unknown ahead of us.

"Captain, I can hardly see in front of me! Please let us turn back!" I heard another crew member argue.

"We have barely started. If we turn back now, we will not be remembered as men but as cowards." I felt bad for saying that, for what kind of captain has to guilt-trip his men into continuing this journey with him. We sailed further and soon I could feel the force of the wind pick up so severely that we were almost blown off the boat entirely. We held on with our lives in what I was sure would be one of our final moments.

One of my men got knocked back so hard that he was slammed into the wall all the way at the other end of the deck, causing him to become unconscious. "Quick! Get him out of here!" I shouted to my crew. Two men grabbed him and helped him back to his quarters, leaving only me and my first mate to combat the ugly storm. He shouted something to me although I could not hear it as the storm grew louder. Then, in one fell swoop I suddenly saw the man fall over the deck of the boat into the cruel and unforgiving waters below us.

I ran to the deck to try and save my friend but by the time I had arrived he must have been at least twenty feet from the boat; therefore, I could not save him. Instead, I had to watch the best man I had brought with me cry for help as he drowned right before my eyes, while I could do nothing to save him. My mates soon returned to the deck, where I had to unfortunately break the tragic news of our friend's disappearance.

"Where is Johnson?" one of them had desperately asked.

"He fell overboard, I believe him to be dead," I tragically told them.

"But how?" they were both quite confused, as Johnson

had proven to be the strongest member of our crew besides myself. Therefore, our hope had somewhat become lost to us. I instructed them to take over their positions as we faced the worst of the storm. Our ship moved back and forth amidst the harsh waves that had begun to make us lose our balance.

"Captain, I believe I see a rock ahead!" the new first mate yelled to me.

"Can we get around it?" I asked him hopefully.

"No, there appears to be no possibility," he replied rather bluntly.

"Then we shall continue as far as we can. Richards, lead us in a prayer, our fate is in God's hands now." So, we prayed as if our lives depended on it because, quite honestly, they did. I went back to the deck to steer the ship myself as I realized that if anyone would lead us out of this life, then, by the heavens, it would be their trusted Captain.

As my crew members covered their eyes with sheer terror I steered as best as I could. The sky had become so dark that I could not see anything. I closed my eyes, dreading what was about to happen, and that's when I heard it. I heard the sound of our boat, our precious girl, crashing against the rock, which left its fair share of damage. "I fear we may not have much longer," a crew mate said as he watched the water pour into the boat.

"Captain, what do we do?"

I paused. What were we to do? If not for my plan for this grand journey we would all have most likely been left unharmed; however, here we stood on a boat that was quite honestly on its last legs. "We must pray. Pray that we live to see tomorrow, my dear friends. Other than that, all we can do is stand here and wait," I said rather bleakly.

"But sir, this was all your idea! We cautioned you that this would happen for some time," one of them said to me.

"I know this, dammit!" I screamed. "Do you think that I am not aware of how much harm this dream of mine has caused? One of our men is dead, another injured beyond repair, and you think I'm not filled with regret?" I continued to ask him.

The two of them just stared at me with despair, as in that moment we all knew that no one on the ship would make it to land alive. As a group we confessed our sins and pleaded to the heavens that we may live in hopes of making a better life for ourselves. The water continued to enter the ship, and it was soon all the way up to our knees. "We're sinking, Captain," one of them so astutely pointed out.

"I know. God have mercy on your souls. I dragged you into this abyss and what have we got to show for it? A broken ship and a lonely crew," I said to them rather bluntly.

The waters eventually became too high for us to bear as our boat continued to sink. I took in one last deep breath before I was taken into the unforgiving sea below me. It came to the point where I could no longer see my crew members and I gave up hope that they were still alive. I swam with all my might and at times I did not think it would be enough. I finally was able to find a rock and managed to pull myself up onto it, wondering whether this was the same rock that had taken our ship down. As I climbed to the top of the rock, I saw the destruction that was in front of me. I turned around to see the land we had so desperately searched for.

I made my return to land alone, my entire crew dead or at the very least lost at sea. I stepped onto the land and while I had imagined this moment to be the proudest moment of my life it happened to be the saddest. While I got to see the new land, was it really worth the cost of my friends? I ask myself this question every night as I see their faces, and I weep, for I know I have the blood of four great men on my hands and, for that, I will forever feel shame.

AUTHOR'S NOTE

There are many people that I would like to thank for what they have done to impact my life. I'll start with my parents, as without them I would have not been able to achieve my dreams. They told me that I could do anything with my life, and they would still be proud of me, and those are words I truly think about every day of my life. I'd also like to thank my grandmother who helped to raise me while I was a child and who helped me to learn more every single day with our long, theological conversations. There are many friends I'd also like to thank, including Nate Whitlock (You'll always be my best friend, buddy), as well as everyone I met during my short period of time in theatre. You all believed in me when I didn't believe in myself and I cannot begin to think of where I'd be without you all, especially Hannah Smithpeters, who helped me to see that writing could be a career option for me. She supported me every step of the way even if I did not show my appreciation as much as I should have. I'd also like to thank Ben Hankinson, Heather Johnson, and Jennifer Little. They have all helped me to learn so much more about who I really am and have inspired me to pursue so many different paths in my life. You were some of the best teachers I ever had the privilege of learning from. Thank you to my cats who have always been a form of emotional therapy for me. Without them, I think that by now I would have most likely gone insane. Finally, I'd like to thank God for giving me such a great support system during my almost 21 years on this Earth. Without him and everyone else listed, there is no way I would have made it as far as I did in life.

This work has taken quite the toll on both my mental and my physical health, as I would commonly lose sleep while writing and would feel a sense of sadness when recalling some of the events from my past. However, if I had the opportunity to do it all over again, I believe that I would not change a thing because what came out of my metaphorical blood, sweat, and tears was a piece of literature that I wound up becoming quite proud of. I thank you for this, reader, as you have given me the opportunity to voice my opinions on various topics. I will leave you with this: If there is one thing I want for you as the reader to take away from this experience, it is to take pleasure in all of the small things that surround your everyday life, whether it be something you find in humanity, nature, or even within yourself. By doing this, you may gain a newfound perspective on life that you otherwise would have entirely missed. Finally, I hope that this book has taught you to pursue your dreams and never doubt yourself because you can make something just as meaningful as what you have read on these pages. I believe in you, and you should believe in yourself too.

Best Wishes,
William H. Adams

www.ingramcontent.com/pod-product-compliance
Lightning Source LLC
Chambersburg PA
CBHW030641190726
48286CB00008B/2612

* 9 7 8 1 9 5 3 9 1 2 8 6 2 *